Glory

Shadow
Tree

jodi lynn

PUFFIN BOOKS

Shadow Tree

PUFFIN BOOKS
Published by Penguin Group
Penguin Young Readers Group,
345 Hudson Street, New York, New York 10014, U.S.A.
Penguin Books Ltd, 80 Strand, London WC2R 0RL, England
Penguin Books Australia Ltd, 250 Camberwell Road, Camberwell, Victoria 3124, Australia
Penguin Books Canada Ltd, 10 Alcorn Avenue, Toronto, Ontario, Canada M4V 3B2
Penguin Books (N.Z.) Ltd, 182-190 Wairau Road, Auckland 10, New Zealand

Published by Puffin Books,
a division of Penguin Putnam Books for Young Readers, 2003

1 3 5 7 9 10 8 6 4 2

Produced by 17th Street Productions,
an Alloy, Inc. company
151 West 26th Street
New York, NY 10001

17th Street Productions and associated logos
are trademarks and/or registered trademarks of Alloy, Inc.

LIBRARY OF CONGRESS CATALOGING-IN-PUBLICATION DATA

Lynn, Jodi.
Shadow Tree / by Jodi Lynn.
p. cm. – (Glory ; 2)
Sequel to: Glory
Summary: Having been expelled from her home in a conservative West Virginia Christian
community, thirteen-year-old Glory struggles to survive in a small town and, though ill,
attempts to realize her dream of traveling to Boston.
ISBN: 0-14-250039-9
[1. Homeless Persons—Fiction. 2. Survival—Fiction. 3. Boston (Mass.)—Fiction.]
PZ7.L9945Sh2003   [Fic]—dc21   2002037084

Printed in the United States of America

FOR TRACI AUTUMN MCCLINTIC

PROLOGUE

Lately I wake up and before I even think where I am—in the woods or in a barn or in my bed back home—I feel this hole aching so big inside, and it feels a lot like panic. And then my brain starts working, and this is what it tells me: I am dying. I will die. In all my years of imagining what my life would be like if I ever left Dogwood, I never imagined this. To be dying at the age of thirteen.

Doesn't it seem like a mistake? Doesn't it seem like God messed up and that some old person somewhere is supposed to die instead of me? I mean, I have nothing against old folks, but isn't that the way life is supposed to work?

I figure it is.

Only, if it's a mistake, I'm the one who made it. I'm the one who committed the sin. God may not have been there for me like he should have, to set it all right, but I deserve my punishment. In fact, I deserve worse.

I can't even say how many times since that night I've asked myself why. Why did I convince my best friend, Katie, to sneak away from everyone with me, to drink spirits even though we knew it wasn't allowed? And why did I go with her to the icy lake afterward and let her walk so far out? Why was I useless when she needed me most, when the ice broke beneath her? It should have been the other way around. I'm the one who should have died that night. That I didn't die is maybe the biggest mistake of all. At least I still have a *little* time left. That's more than Katie has. But God is just. Or so the Reverend back home in Dogwood says. My punishment will ensure I get what's coming to me.

An eye for an eye—that's what the vial of judgment is all about. A punishment to fit the crime, handed down from our ancestors. A poison that gets in your blood and kills you slowly. They made me drink it that night I was banished for what I did to Katie, according to town custom. Sin must be punished in Dogwood, and a sin as grave as mine is punished with banishment and the poison. So now I only have months to live. Three more seasons, if I'm lucky, and already I feel frailer than I've ever been. Like the Reverend said, my symptoms will only get worse as time passes. To the people of Dogwood, I'm already dead. That's what banishment means. Banished from the town and from my family. It was my father himself, as town leader, who made the pronouncement.

So here I am. My family doesn't want me. God doesn't seem to want me. The townsfolk of Dogwood certainly don't want me. And because of the poison, pretty soon life won't want me, either.

You'd think I'd want to curl up and die straightaway, huh? Well, I did, for a while. But I picked myself up and I kept going—away from Dogwood, out into the woods and the unknown. After long, cold days wandering in the snow, half starved and lost to the world, I met Jake—my first-ever stranger. Jake was near my age, and he wasn't at all cruel or scary as the Reverend had warned strangers are. Jake fed me, and kept me warm, and hid me in his parents' barn. He probably saved my life. And then he brought me here, to the nearest town, where his cousin lives. To Shadow Tree.

Part of me still wants to curl up and die. Part of me is all sadness and darkness, where Mama and Daddy and all the others used to be. But then, there is life in me, too—urgent and loud and impatient for me to get moving. And here is why: There is so much to do. There is so much to make up for.

Katie.

We promised each other we'd make it out of Dogwood, into the modern world and all the way to Boston. It was something the town leaders would never allow, on account of the outside being corrupt and sinful and too modern for its own good. But it was the one thing we wanted with all our hearts. So now I've gotta keep the promise for the both of us. It is the only thing I can do to make Katie's death seem like less of a waste. It's my reason for living a little while longer.

CHAPTER ONE

Daddy used to say that the things you're most scared of doing are the ones that need doing most. He said that's part of what helps make you a grown-up. Standing at the edge of town and scared out of my wits, I wondered, *Did that still hold true when you were never gonna get that far?*

For a minute I pictured myself heading back into the woods and living the last of my days off the streams and plants and such out there—just so I wouldn't have to face this big, modern town. At least I *knew* woods.

But of course, turning back wasn't an option. The woods wouldn't get me to Boston. A bus would.

Jake had said I'd need money for my ticket. And to get the money, a job—maybe from his cousin Rebecca. The bus station, and Rebecca, were here. So any way you looked at it, my only way to Boston was through this town, like it or not.

I crossed the road in front of me, continuing on my way deeper and deeper into Shadow Tree.

Before me, the town stretched on and on in a maze of roads and electric lights, big and confusing. The houses had seemed different from the heights of the ridge I'd just come from—like pretty little boxes shining in the dawn. But now they were so big. And there were so many. What's more, I knew there were people inside them. Strangers who could turn out to be any kind of people at all. People who I would have called outsiders, if it wasn't the other way around now.

The Reverend had always warned us that people out here— outside of Dogwood—were godless and deceitful. I now doubted he was right about that. I'd figured out long ago that the Reverend liked to exaggerate and make everything sound worse than it is. But even Jake had warned me of the dangers I might face coming into a real town. He'd said that if people found out I had no home and no parents to tend to me, the "cops" would come get me, and then they'd send me to a place called a Child Welfare Protection Agency, where they'd either track me back to Dogwood or parcel me out to some family of strangers. I couldn't go back to Dogwood—they'd never take me back. I was dead to them, and my heart couldn't bear them turning me away. And I couldn't end up a prisoner to strangers. Both possibilities sent icicles of fear stabbing through me.

Blessedly, I hadn't come upon any strangers here in Shadow Tree yet. Maybe people here started work later than they did at home (folks at home started before dawn), and so they weren't awake now. Maybe most of them didn't even need to work, what with being rich enough to afford these big modern houses. But certainly they'd come outside eventually.

Sure enough, just as the vapor in front of me melted, a figure came out from around a corner ahead. It was a man, tall, bundled from head to toe in a fine, long coat and a fuzzy hat. He held a steaming white cup in his hands and threw a glance in my direction as he walked.

For some reason I froze. Which was a fool idea, I know. The man gave me a curious look, probably because he'd never seen a girl try to act like a statue before. Then he just disappeared behind the opposite corner.

Glory Mason, get ahold of yourself, I thought. This was a town. I was bound to run into some people, for goodness' sake, and trying to become invisible every time I saw one was only gonna make things worse. I didn't know much about strangers—Jake was the only one I'd ever met—but something told me that acting like this would catch their attention quicker than anything else.

Flustered, I wandered in a straight line across street after street, and all around me the town got bigger as I walked. It seemed to grow out of the snowy ground, with the houses of all colors and materials coming closer together the farther I got. The roads, which had been spaced far apart a few minutes before, got wider—with yellow lines in the middle—and they were covered with dirty, wet snow. How could snow get so gloppy and messy?

Screeech! From off to my right, a sound like a—like nothing I could imagine—blasted into my ear. My head snapped around to see what it was, but as I did, someone grabbed the back of my coat and yanked me backward and I went tumbling to the ground with a howl.

"What're you thinking?!"

I blinked, unmoving, then looked up and blinked again. Above me were puffs of white breath, but beyond that, a bearded man squinting down at me. In a flash I was up and backing away. Spinning left and right, I realized a car had stopped a few feet past us, its tracks outlined behind it in the brown slush—slicing right through where I'd been standing.

I turned back and stared at the man with my heart in my mouth. He looked like he was waiting for me to say something. Maybe "thank you." But I didn't know if I should talk to him. Maybe he was a bad man. I couldn't tell just by looking.

He stood there for another second, then shook his head, muttering under his breath as he walked away. My heart slid down through my throat, all the way to my feet. Could he see I didn't belong here? Was he going to tell someone? Without another glance I loped into a half run, half walk away from the scene, heading farther into town.

As I did, more people began to trickle out of their houses and across my path. I tried my best not to meet anyone's eyes. But nobody seemed to notice me at all, besides one or two brief glances, and after a few minutes of realizing this, I slowed down to a walk, lifted my head, and began to look around again.

Was it possible? Could it be that nobody was going to point at me or holler at me or stop me? Of course, it was kind of silly that I was expecting people to know anything much about me just by looking. But then, in Dogwood we would have known a stranger was coming as soon as they reached the town limits. We'd have known it with just one glance. Here, people hardly glanced at all.

As the town around me gradually began to hum with life, the fear that had been zipping up and down my insides all morning started to crumble away, excitement rising up in its place. *A real, civilized town.* I had dreamed of this very thing for so long, and now here it was. Here *I* was. And most important, here was a giant step closer to Boston. So many of those nights when I was starving and dying inside, I had known—just *known*—I'd never make it this far. But I had.

Giddiness took over. My feet took me down one street and then another, my brain and my heart sucking it all in. Then I turned a corner. And when I saw what was in front of me, the hum turned into an explosion.

I'd found the center of town, I guessed.

People dotted the long, wide walkways—women and men and little kids—dressed in hats and scarves and boots of every color and shape imaginable. A few cars swished up and down the roads. Glass-fronted buildings stood everywhere the eye could see. And from where I stood, they went on down two stretches of road at least.

I didn't know where to turn first. I didn't know what to do. There was so much that was new, all at once.

Trembling, I walked up to the window closest to me. It was a store. I knew about such things, though we didn't have need for stores in Dogwood. This one—all of the stores, in fact—seemed to be closed.

In the window was a pyramid made out of shiny red and gold boxes. The box on top was open and held the prettiest candies I'd ever seen—round and smooth, with little heart designs on the top made in pink.

My mouth was watering by now, so I had to turn away and continue on down the row. All the buildings were stores, it seemed, and though they all looked to be closed, I could see through the windows that every one was selling something different—from candy to books to jewelry to doodads of all sorts. Half the stuff I didn't recognize. One store had tables inside and looked like it must serve food. With a pang I was reminded of times with Katie, when we used to pretend we were eating at the fancy Boston restaurants her mama had told us about, ordering everything on the menu.

We'll still do that, Katie, I said silently. *I promise.* But for now, I couldn't handle all the hurt the memory caused. I'd already learned back in the woods that if I let myself sink into the ache inside, I'd never want to get up again. And I didn't intend to let Katie down by my own selfish longing for her. I couldn't let the thought of her leave my mind, but I pushed the sadness part of it to the back and kept walking.

All along the way my mouth kept popping open while I tramped along. I didn't want to look as backward as I felt, but I truly could not imagine where and how and why Shadow Tree came to be filled with all this *stuff.* But then, about halfway down the second street, my mouth snapped shut in surprise. I pulled off a mitten and dug in my pocket once more, pulling out the note Jake had given me. There on the paper was his cousin's name—Rebecca Aiden—and below that, the words *The Rock Shop,* 157 Main Street, Shadow Tree, West Virginia. The very store I was standing in front of now.

I was shocked I'd found it just like that—without even looking. But then, this could only be Main Street. Even I could figure out that if it was called *main,* it meant most of the stores were probably here. More astonishing was that The Rock Shop wasn't anything like its name sounded. I'd imagined a store where you bought rocks to build your cellar with. Or maybe a planting store, like where you could get things to plant around rocks, like ivy or moss, to hold the soil in place. But instead, dazzling before me were scores of gems, bright white electric lights (which were pretty enough on their own) shining down on them so that they sparkled and danced, all laid out on a white velvet cloth. Some were tiny and set in pieces of jewelry like necklaces and rings. Other gems were large and stood alone, sliced like pieces of cake. Some were just in the shape of plain old rocks, only the most beautiful rocks you've ever seen.

The store was closed, like the others, and beyond the display it was dark. I cupped my hands against the glass and tried to peer in, but I already knew that I'd give anything to work in a store like this. If this lady Rebecca would just let me do odd jobs like Jake said, I'd have money saved up soon. Maybe not as soon as I wanted (which was right away), but sooner than never.

When I pulled back from the window, lost in my daydream, I jerked to see a strange girl, skin white as a cloud, with dark hair, staring back at me from inside.

Oh. My bottom lip tightened up into a straight line, and a lump formed in my throat. The girl . . . was me, in a mirror that, I guess, was supposed to be reflecting the rocks. The image froze me solid. There was a single line of dirt curled along my jaw. What bits of my hair weren't tucked under my wool hat were poking out the bottom in long, dark, stringy wisps. And my face was pure white, except for my eyes. They looked huge and lost and out of place against my skin, like the only real live part of the filmy wisp I had become. I scooted back a little, taking in the rest of my upper half in shock. My coat looked like it was hanging on a stick with arms. *I'm a ghost,* flashed through my mind—not for the first time.

Then I turned from the glass and continued back up the street.

Jake had been off his rocker. Seeing myself next to all these beautiful things just went to show it. Who in their right mind, in a fancy store or any store, would give me a job? The only thing I'd be good for around here would be to scare people *away,* but I didn't figure anyone was looking for *that* kind of help.

Stupid stupid stupid, I muttered to myself under my breath. *Glory, you are a fool.*

I was breathing so fast and so hard and suddenly, the air was sucked out of me. I raised my hands to my mouth just in time to muffle a fit of coughing that racked my chest and bent over, leaning against the brick wall of the corner building. I coughed and coughed and kept coughing. I couldn't breathe.

Then, finally, the fit stopped as suddenly as it had come, and I gasped for cold air. I stood up straight, a heavy feeling in my gut. The girl I had seen in the mirror had looked *sick.* She *was* sick. I was sick.

It was fading, my heartbeat was slowing back to normal, but I knew with chilling sureness it would happen again. It would get worse, like the Reverend had said.

A few people were looking at me strange, so I turned toward the nearest window and tried to breathe normally. Slowly the bad feeling inside faded. My mind began to calm.

And when it finally did, I knew what I needed to do next. But I didn't like it.

I forced myself to turn around and go back down Main Street. Then I stood for another minute, looking right and left.

I crossed my arms over my stomach as if to protect myself from whatever was ahead. Then I picked my person. She had a bag in one hand and a child in the other. Any woman with a child couldn't be a kidnapper or a "cop," could she? The way I'd come to picture it, both of these types of demons were big, burly, shifty-eyed men.

Anyhow, surely just *speaking* to her wouldn't do any harm.

Bashfulness and nervousness washed over me, making my ears burn, but I started moving toward her. I tried to remember the manners my mama had taught me—the ones I always used to ignore. *Stand up straight. Say excuse me.*

At the last moment the woman seemed to notice I was coming toward her and looked at me curiously. I swallowed and pulled my shoulders back. Then finally, I did it.

"Excuse me, ma'am," I said. "Can you tell me where the bus station is?"

I'd thought the place would be huge and sprawling. When Mrs. Johansen had explained train stations and bus stations to me and Katie, she'd described them as endlessly big, with people running to and fro, newspapers and coffee in their hands and briefcases where they kept all their important papers.

The Shadow Tree bus terminal turned out to be a tiny building, solid and white, plunked between a large, snow-covered field (no way of knowing what was underneath) and a crowded row of houses. I was far from my nook under the bridge now, all the way across town.

Reaching the front door of the station, I turned toward a sound that had come from behind me. Two kids, maybe nine or ten years old, were kicking an empty glass bottle down the street. The girl was dressed in a pair of dungarees and a tight fluffy brown coat that seemed too small for her. The boy looked unkempt. They stopped at a thin metal gate that stood in front of one of the houses. Then they entered and walked up the front stairs, laughing the whole way.

It was as cold inside the station as the January air was on the outside. A counter stood close to the entrance, with a blue-and-red sign on it that read "Greyhound." A woman stood behind it, tapping away at something I couldn't quite see.

Inwardly, I was praying for a miracle as I approached the counter. Jake had said the money he'd given me wouldn't be enough for a bus ticket, but I was hoping against hope he was wrong. I needed him to be wrong. I had no time to waste looking for some stranger to give me paying work, which would probably never happen, anyway, I now realized. And it was clear I wasn't fit to work for Jake's cousin in her fancy store. So I was hoping and praying that God would give me this one thing, a ticket I could afford.

With not another soul in sight, I took off my hat and waited for the woman to notice me, but she just kept tapping. Finally I cleared my throat.

She looked up then, her big, dark-lidded eyes fluttering as she did. *Oh, Lord!* I'd never seen anyone with so much makeup on. Mrs. Johansen had lipstick that she let me and Katie use once in private, but that was it. Daddy would've skinned my hide if he'd ever found out. I wondered what Daddy would have thought of *this* woman. He would've said she looked just like a jezebel, probably. And I would have gotten mad, because what's so sinful about putting some gunk on your face? But the thought made me long to put my head against Daddy's chest like I used to when I was little and hear the grumble of his voice, grumpy or no. A gruff daddy was better than none.

"Um, excuse me," I said to the jezebel lady. I mentally ran through the story I'd rehearsed on my way down here, realizing suddenly that it seemed far-fetched and foolish. What if I looked too suspicious? What if people my age weren't allowed to buy bus tickets? What if, what if, what if?

"My mama's real sick and she's sending me off to my grandma's in Boston and she wanted me to come down here and see how much a bus ticket costs." I blurted it all out in one breath.

"For when?" the woman asked. She looked bored, much to my relief.

"When?"

"When do you want to go?"

"Um. Soon?"

She met my eyes. *"Soon?"*

I realized how strange that must have sounded, so I tried to cover up. "Well, she wants me to go as soon as I can. So I don't catch it. You know, catch her illness." I cleared my throat again.

"Right." She seemed to be taking me in for the first time, with a sweeping look at my homemade coat and my hand-me-down boots. Then she started tapping once again. I tried not to look too curious about what she was doing. I figured she must be doing figures on a computer, like Jake had talked about. Or was that cash registers you did that on? Was it both?

"Okay. We've got a local that passes through here at 4:12 A.M. Friday mornings."

"Friday?"

"Yep."

"Uh, okay, I mean . . . ma'am, can you please tell me how much it costs?"

"Round-trip?"

I just gnawed my bottom lip and stared at her. I wanted to cry. This was a disaster.

"Are you going in and coming back or just going?"

"Oh, just going." This woman, who would have been by far the strangest person to ever visit our town in all that makeup, was looking at me like I had a pig's tail. If I'd been the old Glory, I would have given anyone who looked at me that way a rude stare right back, but right now I wanted to sink through the floor.

A few more taps and she had a price for me. "One way it's one hundred and sixty-two dollars."

One hundred and sixty-two dollars. Four times as much as Jake had given me. And I'd thought he'd given me so much! I did the math in my head. I needed one hundred and twenty-two more dollars. Jake had warned I'd need more than forty, but I'd never imagined so *much* more. Where on earth was I going to get that kind of money?

"Um, she didn't give me enough money, I guess," I sputtered as I backed away. "I'll come back later."

I turned away from her heavy glance and headed for the door.

Back out on the street, the sun was melting away some of the snow, sending it in little brown dribbles down the sides of the roads. I didn't know where I was headed, but I was walking fast, my nails digging into my palms. I wanted to punch something.

"Unfair unfair unfair," I muttered to myself under my breath. *Unfair!*

I knew I'd resolved not to expect anything from God anymore, but couldn't He have mercy on me just once? Couldn't He help me do this one thing, after all the sadness He'd let my life turn into? I felt like Job in that old Bible story, when God lets the devil take everything away from him—his family, his health—just to prove to the devil that despite all the hardships, Job would be loyal to God, anyway. When my older sister,

Teresa, taught that story to us in Bible study, she said it was supposed to help us learn to praise the Lord no matter what. But it always made me mad. And now I wanted to scream. Where was I going to come up with one hundred and twenty-two dollars? It might as well have been a million!

Just to make myself feel worse, I started thinking of all the things I wanted to do when I got to Boston and how I wasn't going to get to do any of them. I wasn't going to make it. I was going to die in my stupid little nook under the bridge.

I walked aimlessly for a while, making circles up and down the streets. It was the only way to get out all the anger inside and also to keep warm—since I had nowhere to go except back out of town.

Now that I was paying attention, I noticed that the town took on different personalities every few blocks. On some streets the houses were built almost on top of each other, some with signs that said "For Sale" and all the windows dark. Then, a few streets beyond, there would be houses the size of palaces (or at least they seemed like palaces to me) with dripping gables and little terraces everywhere and ornate drapery hanging inside. I saw what the Reverend meant by "the greed of the outside world." Not that I wouldn't want to live in one of those big, fine houses myself—or at least set foot in one—but it certainly didn't seem fair to everybody else.

I wandered past stores—some fancy, some not so fancy,

depending on where they were placed. I wandered past a large field with trees dotted fetchingly here and there. A sign said it was called Apple Blossom Park. At least all of these sights distracted me a little.

Back near Main Street there were even more people out now, and the stores were all open. Folks ducked in and out of them, talking, sometimes laughing through their scarves. It was all very interesting and amazing to see. But I couldn't help thinking that amidst all these people, I felt even more lonely than I had that morning. I'd always imagined my first trip into the modern world as being swept into it all. Of course, I'd always imagined it happening in Boston, with Katie, amongst thick crowds and dreamy, impossibly tall buildings. But here I just felt locked out—like I could only watch these lives hustling back and forth, but I couldn't be a part of them. I didn't know anybody here. I couldn't stay here, and I didn't have the money to get away. I had no place in this town to go to and nobody seemed to notice, and even though I was relieved about that, it made me feel even more alone.

No bus ticket, no work, no anything. After all the planning and daydreaming and hoping, nothing in this outside world, in this *life,* was turning out as I'd expected.

Nothing.

CHAPTER
TWO

I was just in the middle of kicking a chunk of ice out of my way when I sensed a building in front of me and looked up from the tips of my boots. The sign said "Pete's Get and Zip." A teenage girl, only a couple of years older than me by her looks, had just stepped out the right-hand door with a brown sack in her arms. I could see a bunch of bananas poking out of the top. I love bananas.

How on earth a store could get bananas this time of year, I did not know. Back home, Daddy and Mr. Johansen had always gotten them with the summer shipments as a treat, but never in the winter. Then again, Mr. Johansen did come back from one of his trips to the outside with a sack of oranges once. Mama and Mrs. Johansen had about eaten their shoes, they were so excited.

Maybe since this man Pete was rich enough to own a store, he was also rich enough to get bananas shipped from South America or wherever. Maybe they came in a special airplane. All I knew was that I wanted some, bad. A couple of bananas couldn't cost that much, could they?

Forgetting about my appearance, I stepped inside, and immediately I felt my bad mood evaporate. The store was toasty and warm, and the whole place smelled like roasting chicken, which is an even better smell than fresh coffee and flapjacks. I pulled off my hat, rubbing my ears to get them warmed up, and stamped my boots. I didn't really get a good look at the place till afterward. And when I did, I couldn't believe my eyes.

From wall to wall and from floor to ceiling, there was before me more food than the entire village of Dogwood could have eaten in all the hundred and thirty-two years it had existed. There were boxes and cans with the most divinely colorful words and pictures on them and vegetables of every kind. There were fruits as shiny as new pennies, glistening with drops of dew. I knew I shouldn't gawk and make myself look backward, but this . . . this was amazing.

The first thing I did was head for the bananas. I picked up a bunch and held it against my nose. They smelled like summer. I looked at the price—only fifty-nine cents for one pound. I peeled two off the bunch and slid my feet down the row to a mound of apples. They were only eighty-nine cents for a pound. It wouldn't hurt to get a few of those, too.

I glanced over several items I didn't recognize until my eyes alighted on the collard greens. At the sight of them I wrinkled up my nose. But Mama always said they were good for you, and I thought half achingly, half hopefully that maybe they'd help to slow down my getting sick. I picked up a bunch. I got two potatoes, too, then hurried to the next row.

I'd started out sensible, but by the time I got through all five rows, I'd gone a little crazy on items. I had three bags of noodles, a sealed packet of ham, and a box of oatmeal, plus three cans of green beans and two cans of red, all piled up in my arms on top of what I already had. Plus a gadget called a Swiss Army knife that I decided I couldn't live without. (Can opener . . . scissors . . . All-Purpose Swiss Army knife is what the package said.) And a bar of soap that didn't look at all like soap back home and smelled like lilacs (the memory of my dirty face in the glass had made up my mind).

By my math it should all add up to eighteen dollars and thirty-five cents. It was a lot, but I needed to eat to keep healthy, didn't I? Especially now.

I headed up to the front of the store, where it looked like you had to pay. A woman was already in line. I didn't notice her at first, so absorbed was I by the store and all its goods, but then I realized she was wearing some heavenly-smelling perfume, and it made me turn to look at her more closely. Her long dark hair was pulled into a knot in the back, and she wore a filmy, purple dress with white scrolls snaking down the back in flowery patterns all the way to her ankles. A belt was knotted about her waist, and it was the same color as the piece of cloth that held back her hair. She had a red basket in her hand and was unloading the last of her food from it. Why hadn't I gotten one of those? My arms were sore.

I guess she must have felt me staring because all at once she jerked around to look at me. Her front was just as pretty as her back. She had on a nice pink lipstick, but not too much like the lady at the bus station, and her eyes were a soft, soft brown. I don't know why, but somehow I felt like having her looking at me was just like being squeezed in a hug.

She looked down at my arms, then up to my face.

"Here you go." She moved some of her things to make room for me to put down my armload, and my muscles thanked me as I did. When I met her eyes again, she was giving me a strange look, but then she smiled and nodded down at the pile.

"I've always wanted to do that, too," she said. "Take only the bananas I want instead of the whole big bunch. My kids won't touch them, and they always end up going bad. But I've never had the nerve to take just a couple. Good for you."

I felt my face glowing bright red. The lady and the man at the register were both looking at me now.

"Oh, don't encourage her, Bobbie," the man said, but he was smiling. "They're supposed to be sold in bunches."

Then the lady—Bobbie, I guessed—actually winked at me as she leaned in to pay. Her perfume, it was jasmine, I think, breezed over my face. "He'll make an exception for you, sweetie."

The man sighed and then, with a crinkle of paper and a "Thanks, Pete," she turned and left.

*   *   *

My nook under the bridge, where Jake had left me early that morning, was pretty much as I'd left it: smelly and overgrown with wet moss, but now it was drippy from the melting snow, too. Still, this was the closest thing I had to a home, and I was relieved to see it.

After I'd put down my bags, I plodded off into the woods a little ways off and began gathering firewood. It was a slow task because of the snow everywhere and my cranky mood, on account of being so hungry, and it took me a good fifteen minutes of poking around to find some wood that was mostly dry. I had to peel a lot of bark off the nearby trees to get any kind of good kindling.

I was making my way back to the nook when all at once something caught the corner of my eye. A bit far off my path to the west, just beyond a stand of pine trees, was a clearing, and from what I could see, it was filled with all sorts of things. Hunks of metal and tin and who knew what else, in all sorts of shapes and size. It even looked like there was a car back there. It looked abandoned, but I couldn't imagine that could be true. People didn't throw away cars, did they? Must be somebody's property, I figured.

Anyway, I was starving, so I wasn't going anywhere right then, except to get some food ready. I went to my bag and pulled out the things I wanted to eat. A banana, a few slices of meat, the beans. I tried to forget that my first journey into town had been so terribly disappointing. It wasn't as if I'd really expected to fit in here, but somehow I hadn't realized just how badly I would stick out. And I was no closer to finding work, or buying a bus ticket, or reaching Boston. But right now I couldn't think about any of that. I just had to make this fire.

Luckily Jake had had the good sense to give me matches, and I used them now to light the kindling I'd gathered, which took ages. As the fire finally leapt into action, though, I had time to think of that lady, the one at the grocery store—Bobbie. Something about her was so comforting. Maybe there *were* mostly kind people out here in the world, like Katie and I'd always imagined. Maybe I'd just think about that instead of how on earth I was gonna get where I needed to go. And get there quick, for that matter.

I was up before dawn the next morning. It was a combination of the dripping walls and the moldy smell and memories that made it so when I woke up to take care of nature in the woods, I couldn't get back to sleep. I started up my fire and made a mug of pine needle tea and wondered when the sun would rise and make all the night's dreams seem like just that, only dreams.

Pulling my knees up to my chest, I set the mug right under my chin so I could feel the warm moisture on my face and closed my eyes. They hadn't been bad dreams. Katie was in all of them I could remember, and nothing real special happened. They were just these visions of Katie and me sitting in my room, on my creaky old bed back home; sharing a jar of lemonade and laughing;

Katie sitting on a countertop and throwing flour at my face. They'd been happy dreams. Too happy.

Waking up afterward—that was the bad part. It made me feel the shock of Katie being gone all over again, and the shock of my banishment and having to leave my family, and the shock of being headed for the grave myself. And the longer I sat, the bigger the black hole twirling around inside me got. So I was glad when the first rays of light peeked over the rise, signaling it was finally time to get up and go. I didn't know what I'd do today, but I knew I couldn't stay here and drown in my memories.

On my way down the hill, I circled around the spot I'd seen last night, where all the strange piles of rusted tin and metal were, just to pass the time till the sun was fully up. I could clearly see a rusty old red car standing—more like stooping—in the open space nearest me. A pile of wheels leaned against its front.

I took a few more steps forward, trying to make out as much as I could in the gray light. As I did, a *crunch* sounded through the still air, coming from the opposite end of the clearing. I froze. Whatever it was on the other side, if there was anything there, froze, too. I waited and breathed, but nothing. I dared to scratch an itch on the edge of my nose, and still nothing moved. Finally I got up the courage to back away, one silent step at a time. When I was far enough that I couldn't even see the tip of the rusty red car anymore, I let out a sigh of relief and turned downhill. It had just been an animal, I figured. Or my imagination. But still, I felt spooked the whole way to town.

Shadow Tree hardly seemed less strange than it had the day before. I wondered if it was partly the cold that made everything appear so big and far off, as if a layer of ice covered it all to keep me on the outside. I longed to go into one of the stores along Main Street, to be a part of the warmth and business and bustle that everyone else seemed to be part of, but one glance at my clothes, and a memory of my appearance in the shop window mirror the day before, and I remembered why I couldn't. I even felt embarrassed now for showing myself in that grocery store.

Maybe one of the stores on the outskirts of town—the ones that had been less fancy—would give me some work.

But even as I was planning on heading elsewhere, my feet took me back to the front window of The Rock Shop, as if an invisible hand was pulling me there.

Yep, Jake was crazy. But now that I'd realized getting work here was out of my reach, the store looked even more appealing. It was open this time. I could see a girl in the back of the store, maybe a few years older than me, standing behind the counter and writing on a piece of paper. Every once in a while she'd stop what she was doing, pick at one of her fingernails, then begin writing again. I wondered if she was Rebecca. I also wondered how she could look so bored surrounded by so much beauty. But then, hadn't I felt the same way so many times, surrounded by the blazing hills back home? I wished somebody had come and shaken me and said, "Wake up, Glory Mason! You won't have this forever." I wished I could do the same for this girl.

Maybe I could just go in and *look*. Did they have laws saying some people could look and some couldn't? I didn't think so. I wouldn't have to talk to the girl or anything. I could just walk in, have a peek around, and walk out. It looked so warm inside— the girl was wearing only a T-shirt. What was to stop me?

Despite the bitter cold I pulled off my hat and mittens and smoothed my hair, but all it did was stick to my hands. Looking right to left to make sure no one was watching, I licked my palms and tried it again. This time the hair stayed down. I ran a sleeve across my face but couldn't bear to look in the mirror again. I just hoped I looked halfway decent. Then I opened the door.

The jingle that followed made me jump back a step, and the door almost swung closed again in front of me. I managed to slide in before it did and looked up to see some bells attached there at the top. *Oh.*

I could also see that I'd already attracted attention. The girl at the counter was looking at me with a mix of curiosity and amusement.

"Hi," I managed to choke, putting my hands up to my cheeks. If my face hadn't been red from the cold, it was certainly red now.

"Can I help you with something?" the girl asked. I wished

she'd go back to picking her nails. And besides, I hadn't expected for her to ask to help me. Was I only supposed to come in here if I wanted to buy something?

"Um, I'm looking for . . ." *For what, for what?* "Gems . . ."

The girl lost her look of curiosity. It was replaced by a look of decision. She had finally decided that I was a fool.

"What kind?"

I looked about the room furiously. What kind of gems were there in the world? Diamonds, I knew, but those were the most expensive, weren't they? Rubies? Emeralds?

Finally my eyes alighted on a counter and a small sign.

"I'm looking for some ahh-gah-tee? Do you have any?"

"Aah-get," she repeated, pronouncing it the correct way. "Sure. We have a few different colors. And then there's Brazilian, Uruguayan, or . . . is this for Valentine's Day?"

I didn't hear what she was saying anymore for at that moment—in an attempt to get closer to the Agate sign for a clue—I banged my shoulder against a glass shelf, and gems of every size and shape began to scatter and fall.

"Oh, I'm sorry!" I squeaked, but before I could even regain my balance, she was out from behind the counter and on her knees, picking up the pieces.

"You know, if you break something, you have to pay for it," she snapped, sending a thread of panic snaking down into my belly.

"Sara, that's enough."

The girl, Sara, and I both looked up to see a woman standing in a doorway behind the counter.

It wasn't just any woman, though.

It was the woman from the grocery store.

She seemed to recognize me at the same time I did her. Her eyes opened a little wider. "Head on into the back room, please, Sara."

The girl, Sara, suddenly looked embarrassed. She nodded slowly and was gone quicker than a blink.

"I'm sorry about that. Sara's been studying for exams, and I think she's a little stressed out."

When I failed to reply, since all I could think to do was stand there staring, Bobbie stuck out her hand. "We've met before. I'm Rebecca."

Rebecca? *Rebecca?* I was too confused to speak. But luckily my manners took over. I put my hand in hers and shook.

"I'm Glory," I said. "Pleased to meet you, ma'am." I had never said this sentence before in my life. It felt strange on my lips and silly.

"Likewise, Glory. It seems we have no choice, anyway, but to meet. Looks like fate."

"Fate?"

"Ohhh, whatever." She rolled her eyes as she waggled both hands at her sides, as if to shake off the subject. "I just like to believe there's no such thing as a coincidence. But who knows? Maybe it's just this town's so small that everybody can't avoid meeting everybody else."

I tried to understand that she was calling this town small. Jake had called it small, too, but I couldn't make sense of how that could be possible. Meanwhile Rebecca was standing there staring at me expectantly. And I realized part of why this was so confusing.

"But that man at the grocery. He called you . . . Bobbie."

Rebecca squinted for a second, then her eyes brightened. "Oh, Pete. That's what he calls me. After Bob Dylan. He's my favorite."

"Oh." I would have wondered who Bob Dylan was, but I was too busy trying to understand that this woman and Jake's cousin were one and the same lady.

"You can call me Becky, honey. I wouldn't have forgotten you, anyway. You were quite a sight with all that food in your arms. Do you live around here?"

"Mmmm, huhh, just outside of town. Up the hill. Well, a ways out of town, actually."

Rebecca nodded, her eyes squinting up again. We both stood there silently staring at each other.

"Well," I said.

"Well," she replied, rubbing her hands together and folding one over the other.

I took a step backward. I guess this was where I was supposed to say again that it was mighty nice meeting her and get on out before I knocked over anything else. But the thought of heading back into the cold, and out of this woman's presence, was the last thing I wanted to do.

I chewed on my bottom lip. What did I have to lose? If she said no, I'd be no worse off than I was now. And if I didn't do it now, I never would. I braced myself to be mortified. Then I sucked in my breath.

"Can I have a job?" I blurted out, the question coming out in one breath. Becky's eyebrows almost shot clear off her forehead. I couldn't believe the words had actually come out of me, though I'd always been known back home for saying what was on my mind. I also couldn't believe what Becky did next—which was laugh.

"Well, you're a forward thing, aren't you? What do you need a job for? You couldn't be more than . . ."

"Thirteen," I finished for her. Then without another breath I forged ahead, telling her how I could work anytime at all and giving her my made-up story about having a sick ma. Only I added a part about needing to earn some money to buy bus passage to Boston, where I was gonna live with my grandma for a while. I felt awful lying, but what choice did I have? And I knew better than to tell her Jake had driven me here and told me to talk to her, for fear that if she did get suspicious of my story, she might trace my trail all the way back home.

While I spoke, Becky's look of amusement turned into a seriousness that I couldn't read, and then suddenly we were again standing in an awkward silence. I didn't know what to make of it. She was obviously thinking, but thinking what?

"You don't have a choice, huh, but to earn some money?"

"No, ma'am." I could tell she wanted me to say more, but if I tried to tell one more lie, I'd choke on it.

"And your mother can't take care of you?"

"No, ma'am." This, at least, was the truth.

"Well." Becky's brown eyes softened back again into warm friendliness. "I'm sure you know that technically, you're supposed to be sixteen to work."

My hopes fell in an instant. I looked at my boot tips and willed back the disappointed ache inside.

"But you know," Becky hurried on, putting her hand on my shoulder, "it'd only be temporary, right? I've been thinking I need someone to help in the back room. Sorting this big load of rocks we got in recently. And we're backed up on sending out newsletters and stuff. You think you could do that?"

"Yes, ma'am." I nodded furiously.

"Well, I can't afford more than part-time help, and I can't pay much—five dollars an hour. Would you still want it?"

"Oh, yes, ma'am." I nodded again. Five dollars for one hour's work seemed like a fortune! And any time was better than none, no matter how many hours "part-time" added up to.

"Well, then," Becky said, looking me up and down. "I don't suppose you have references."

I shook my head.

"It'd have to be on a trial basis, then. You know, to try each other out. . . . But as long as that's all right . . . you've got the job."

Before I knew what I was doing, I'd thrown my arms around Becky and planted a big kiss on her cheek.

"Thank you, ma'am!" When I pulled away, Becky took one look at me and grabbed a tissue from off the counter. I noticed then what she'd already noticed, that there were tears in my eyes. But she didn't say anything about it.

"There's one condition," she said as I sniffed and wiped. "You really have to call me Becky. Ma'am makes me feel old."

"All right."

"I've got Sara Mondays, Wednesdays, and Fridays in the evenings after school, and Saturday mornings, obviously, so what if you come by after school Tuesdays and Thursdays?"

"Oh, I don't go to school," I blurted out.

Becky's eyebrows shot up. "What do you mean, you don't go to school? But you're only thirteen."

I watched the concern fill Becky's face, feeling my own heart start to pound. I'd forgotten about school. Jake had said everybody was supposed to go to one. In Dogwood we'd only had to go till age eleven. *Think, think.* Then I remembered that he'd said his parents had wanted to home teach him, but he had begged and pleaded to go to a school with other kids. It was the best I had. "I get home taught," I ventured, watching Becky's face, which was unreadable. "I can study on the days I don't work."

She looked at me, squinting a little.

"I'm sure it'll be fine with my mama," I added nervously. "Just as long as I get all my work done."

Now Becky nodded slowly, but her eyes had a faraway look. "Well, then, I can use you for the whole day Tuesdays and Thursdays. We open at nine and close at five. Okay?"

"Yes, ma'—Becky."

"Good. All right, honey. I'll see you then."

"Bye, ma'am. Becky. Thank you."

She just nodded again before I turned and jingled out the door.

On my way back uphill I went over the whole amazing conversation in my head. I thought about my performance, the lies about my mama and school and such, and figured I'd done a pretty good job. I thought about how nice Becky smelled, and how kind she seemed, and how she'd talked about fate. Most of all, I thought about Boston. I thought about how, if God just gave me long enough to live, I was going to make it there. And Katie was going to look down and see.

Becky had said I shouldn't pay any mind to it, but maybe she was right. Maybe something bigger than me or her had brought us together.

Maybe God was looking out for me after all.

CHAPTER THREE

Have you ever been so happy about something that it made you sad? It's an odd thing. I don't know why it works out that way—I guess it's because you start hoping for so much that the hope gets too big to be inside you. And then you realize it won't last.

Sitting at my fire that night with everything around me aglow in white moonlight, I tried to bask in my day's success, but it only filled me with an ache. It made me think about wolves howling at the moon. That's how having hope, and knowing I shouldn't and couldn't keep it, made my heart feel. Like howling out of longing for the beauty of the world.

What right did I have to get so excited about something, as if Katie had never even died? And for that matter, what right did I have to long for things that Katie would never have because of me and what I'd done? How could life go on, even for a little while, with her gone?

A shiver ran through my body, and I threw some more wood onto the fire.

The answer was, it couldn't. I couldn't remember a time that I hadn't had Katie in my life. My mama and her mama had nearly raised us as sisters, relying on each other to tend to one or both of us as if we were their own. There wasn't a time I didn't have Katie to talk to, or hug, or run to when I was vexed or downright fuming or just getting my feelings hurt. I wasn't me without her.

With that thought, I leaned back and moved my hands to place them over my heart, but as I did, my breath left me. Suddenly I was coughing, bent over my knees, trying to get air into my lungs. For several moments I struggled like this, till finally the worst was past. When I finally sat up and wiped my brow to get my hair out of my eyes, my skin was slick with sweat.

I sat for a minute, panting, remembering when this had happened yesterday. *Please don't let it take me this quickly,* I thought. *Please, give me time.*

A few more minutes passed, and I felt sure enough that the fit was over to stand up. I looked around, at a loss—scared and sick to my stomach. The thought of dying was blinding me all at once; it filled up the inside of my body like some kind of sickness all its own.

Though it was nighttime, the moon lit everything around me brilliantly. The ache inside was unbearable. Maybe I could head over to the clearing and get a better look at all that stuff, under cover of night. Something to get my mind occupied and to stop this misery.

I wove through the trees, the snow reflecting a clear white path before me. The forest rustled softly in the cold breeze, and an owl *whoo-whooed* from somewhere above. It felt like something out of a scary story.

Katie came back to my mind, younger—maybe age seven or eight. Back then when she'd sleep over, we'd stay in the same bed and tell each other scary stories that weren't really scary at all, and we'd fall asleep holding hands. Her cheeks were chubbier then, and she was taller than me. I'd spurted up the following year, but even after that, she'd said that I still had a "short-Glory" personality. Like I wanted to make up for being a small person by showing people they couldn't tell me what to do—even after I'd grown tall as her brother Thomas.

Up ahead, the pines thinned out, and then there they were—the bulky shapes glinting in the moonlight. I walked cautiously again, but no noises stopped me this time, and I soon found myself on the edge of the clearing—coming up right next to a big square . . . stove. It was the electric kind that I'd seen through Jake's kitchen window. All around there were rubber wheels and piles of papers, soggy and moldy from the damp. There were old radios and big soft chairs with the seats ripped out and hunks of metal that didn't really look like anything. And of course, there was the car I'd spotted before. The whole place was even eerier than it had been that morning but also too enticing to walk away from. I'd never seen half of these contraptions, and now they were all gathered here in one place for me to explore.

Most unbelievable of everything, it all seemed to be unwanted.

Tall grass poked out of the snow and grew up all around undisturbed, meaning most of this stuff had been here for a long while. Rust and mold and decay had taken over. People had actually thrown these things *away*. No one in Dogwood would ever do such a thing—the Reverend often preached about the evils of wasting those gifts that God had bestowed.

Now that I was out of the woods, the world around me seemed perfectly quiet except for my footsteps crunching in the snow as I wandered in circles, picking up this and that, heedless of what critters might be hiding beneath. I read the words—*Black & Decker, La-Z-Boy*—were those the names of the owners? I pressed the levers and knobs. Nothing worked, but I didn't mind.

After I'd exhausted my curiosity with everything else, I walked up to the car—which I'd wanted to save till last—and ran a hand over the back end. A few chunks of paint came off in my hand. The word *Lincoln* was scrawled just above some broken glass that had once covered some kind of lightbulb.

I slowly made my way around to the side. I didn't know why, but I felt like this car was sacred, and I wanted to take it in slowly. Through the windows I could see a big seat in the back, large enough to sleep a person or two. The front was filled with dried leaves and what all. Mold was creeping up the side door, and the wheel for steering (like I'd seen in Jake's car) was gone.

I ached for this car. It had once been shiny and new. Somebody had driven it and gone places with it and maybe had conversations in it and now it was just here alone, rusted and torn up and forgotten.

It was a discard, just like me. It was alone, and so was I.

My heart howled at the moon. I laid my head against the top of the car and cried.

At first light I was back at the clearing. With a plan, and with all my earthly possessions in tow. Luckily the morning wasn't as cold as the past few had been, and I knew soon enough I'd work up a sweat.

First I began clearing the area directly around Lincoln (that's what I'd decided to call it). I yanked up the tall strands of grass, patting the snow down with my boots, until I'd made a decent entranceway and a place for a fire—close enough to lend warmth to the car. Then I opened all four doors and began digging out all the rubbish. Sticks and leaves and dirt and garbage came sifting out into little piles, which I raked away with a big flat board.

Once the back and front seats were clear, I scavenged around for rags and found an old blanket that would do the job perfectly. I used it to scrub the inside of the doors and the windows. Occasionally I picked up a handful of snow and rubbed it into the cloth to make it wet enough to wash away the dirt—not perfect, but it made the car cleaner. I wished I had some ammonia to scrub away the mold, but all I could do was rub at it real good until most of it came off.

Around noon I rested on a nearby pile of tires and ate some snacks. Then I went in search of something to make curtains. If anybody did come around this place, I wanted to be hidden. And besides, curtains would make it feel a little more cozy. I found a large green tarp that wasn't too dirty, and after I'd scrubbed the mold off its slick surface, I tore it into sections with my knife. With bits of wire I attached the sections so that two hung over every window like curtains. I could even tie them back if I wanted with smaller, longer strips.

It took me all morning and half the afternoon, but finally the car was ready.

Yanking all of my things—my knapsack, my groceries—into the backseat with me, I pulled all the doors closed. There. It wasn't so bad; it was kind of nice. With a fire so close and my own body heat, it would warm up, and anything was better than sleeping under that drippy, moldy bridge.

The seats still needed work. There were springs inside them, and one of them was poking at my behind. The front seats were ripped. I'd have to cover them, but the tarp wouldn't do—it was too crunchy and slippery. Maybe I'd find something in town, on my way to the store.

Feeling uplifted by both of those prospects, I began to unpack and divided the space into sections as I did. The backseat would be my bed, where I'd put one of my two coats and the blanket Jake had given me to keep me warm at night. The front, on the side where the steering wheel should have been, would be the pantry. I unloaded all my small stock of food into stacks on the cushion, setting the cheese up on a ledge under the front window, where it would stay cooler.

The other front side would be where I kept the things that were most important. I found a little compartment that folded open and I stashed my money there, my log of the money I owed Jake, my matches, and my knife. On the ledge above I carefully laid out my only sentimental possessions: the picture of my family that Mama had slipped in my pocket before I left and the note Jake had written me. The Mason family was smiling out from the photo as always, unaffected and unknowing of how far they had traveled in my pocket. I kissed my pinky and touched each face with it—Teresa, Mama, Daddy, Theo. I had to imagine kissing baby Marie's face, too, since she wasn't born in time for the photo. Then I set the precious picture down.

Once it was all done, I sat back and surveyed my work, feeling strangely satisfied. I didn't have much of anything, but for now at least I could claim this car as my own little space in the world, and I had done it all myself. It felt like a slice of home.

Home. Despite everything that had happened, I pictured my house—where the kitchen was always extra warm with baking, where there was a fire in the fireplace all winter long and usually somebody sitting by it sewing. I pictured my own room, with the gauzy curtains and the faded blue walls and the window right by my bed that always showed me a view of the barn lot and a chicken or two.

Now I was getting excited about living in a lonely old car in the woods? Never again would I have Mama or Daddy to make a place a home for me. They'd never be there to make me get up in the morning or yell at me for not doing enough work. I was my own mama and daddy now.

I remembered Daddy's talks with me about responsibility; which was one of the most important virtues us kids in Dogwood were raised with. Since everybody shared equally, one do-less (according to folks in town, that person would be me) could make things harder on everybody else, and it wouldn't be fair or right.

But now I only had responsibility for me, Glory Mason, and nobody else. And as nice as that would have sounded to me once—to be on my own and not have to please anyone else—now it just felt . . . empty. How would I know how to make the right decisions? How would I fix things and figure out things without Mama or Daddy to help?

I sighed, my shoulders shuddering and seeming extra bony and small. Well, like it or not—prepared or not—I'd have to figure it out. If that was what I needed to do to get to Boston, I'd have do it.

There was one thing I liked about myself, at least. Folks in town had always called it stubbornness. It was the fact that once I set my mind to something, I wouldn't give up.

CHAPTER
FOUR

By the clock in the town square I had fourteen minutes to go. I watched the minute hand tick away, mouthing the numbers.

"Glory?"

I whirled around to the sound of Becky's voice. She was standing there, wrapped in a pretty patchwork coat, her dark hair tucked under a purple hat and her mouth covered by a scarf.

"What're you doing standing all the way over here?"

I didn't know whether or not to explain that I didn't have a watch to tell me when nine o'clock came around. I definitely knew not to explain that I'd already been standing here for twenty-three minutes.

It didn't seem to matter, though, because as I stood stumbling over the right words Becky curved her arm through mine and started pulling me along Main Street, toward number 157. Toward The Rock Shop and my new job.

"Don't look so worried," Becky said, leaning her head in toward mine. "I like that you're early. You're punctual. That's unusual for a girl your age." The idea of me being punctual would have made me laugh if it hadn't meant remembering home, because of all the times I'd been hollered at for being late.

Becky rattled the key in the door with one hand as she pulled off her hat with the other, and then with a jangle we were inside. A square on the wall with lots of buttons on it was buzzing away, but Becky seemed to take this as a matter of course. I watched with curiosity as Becky tapped at a few of the buttons, and the buzzing stopped.

"My daughter, Amelia—she's about your age—wouldn't get out of bed early if there was a four-alarm fire and her survival depended on it."

I gave a timid little half laugh. I wondered what Becky's daughter was like. I wondered if she looked like her mother and if she was as nice. I also felt a tiny pang of jealousy. She probably had a great life.

Becky was fiddling with switches all over the room, turning on this and that electric light. I'd never seen anyone switch on a light before, but as usual (at least lately) I made a point not to gawk. I'd have to watch that.

As I began to pull off my outer layers, I felt a wave of self-consciousness, even stronger than normal. There was a small mountain stream by my clearing, and this morning I'd stripped down and splashed myself with freezing cold water, then scrubbed as hard and fast as I could with a piece of cloth and the soap I'd bought, even as goose bumps covered every inch of my body from the cold. I was now wearing my best clothes—a sweater and a pair of pants that had belonged to Jake's mama, both too small for me. I felt awkward and not as clean as I would have liked.

"I . . . I like your coat," I said stupidly, grasping at the only conversation I could think of to divert attention off of my appearance.

Becky looked down at her coat. "Oh, thanks. It cost a fortune, but I just fell in love."

I stared at her dumbly. A fortune? But it looked like she'd made it herself.

"My kids tell me it looks like a sleeping bag. C'mon, I'll show you where you'll be working." I followed Becky through the doorway at the back.

Oh. The back room didn't look nearly as fancy as the front of the store. It was just a square room with white walls and a desk with lots of papers on it. In one corner there was a wide wooden table, covered in all sorts of rocks and tools, and beside it, a washbasin.

I couldn't help feeling disappointed. But then something on the desk caught my eye.

"You've got a radio!"

Becky, who'd been hanging her coat on a hook by the door, paused. *Watch yourself, Glory.*

"You like music that much?" she asked.

I nodded.

"Well, then, we can take turns picking. Although I have to warn you, I don't like rap or heavy rock or anything like that. Especially none of the violent stuff."

I had no idea what she was talking about, but I said, "Me either."

Becky leaned over a white device of some sort with a glass pitcher resting on it and flicked a switch. Curiously, it started bubbling and sputtering.

"Anyway, honey, this is where we do our calls and our paperwork." She nodded at the desk. "We do a lot of sorting and washing and polishing, too, mostly on the less expensive stones, so that's what the work area is for." She walked over to the table next to the basin and picked up a handful of stones of various colors, covered in dirt.

"Basically that's where we make *these* look like some of what's out there."

Becky tilted her head to indicate the front room, then leaned forward and held out her hand. I opened mine beneath it, palm up, and she handed me the rocks. Looking at them, I found it hard to believe they could become as shiny and beautiful as the ones displayed in the front room. And the thought that making that happen would be part of my job seemed too lovely to be real.

"Don't worry," Becky said, seeming to realize what I was thinking once again. "I'll show you how to do it. And we'll start you out slow and on the lowest-grade stock so if you mess up, it's no big deal. Believe it or not, there are beautiful stones hiding inside all these rocks. It's just a matter of uncovering them."

By the time five o'clock rolled around, my brain felt like mush and my hands *looked* like mush. The glass pitcher, it turned out, was for brewing coffee, and it'd been filled all day, but Becky hadn't offered me any, and I felt too bashful to ask.

I'd messed up with the desk work. I mean, *really* messed up. Becky had asked me to stuff papers into some envelopes and mail them while she was out front. I'd put them in the envelopes fine—I'd seen a few of them in my life, mostly belonging to Katie's mama. I'd even figured out I was supposed to lick them to make them stick. Then I'd carried them out to the blue mailbox down Main Street like she'd asked me. But when I came back, she looked upset. Apparently I was also supposed to put these little sticky squares of paper, called stamps, on them. And Becky had found the ones that I'd been supposed to use still sitting on the desk.

So while she closed the store and ran down to the post office to explain and get them to open the mailbox, she told me to start washing the stones and keep an eye on the phone. Now, I knew I was gonna mess the phone thing up, but I didn't know how to tell her. I knew what a phone was, but I'd never been up close to one till today.

Then suddenly she was gone and it was too late to tell her anything, and a ringing came from under the papers. The first few times I just pretended to myself that I didn't hear it. I went into the bathroom and closed the door, hoping to drown out the sound. And that was fine for a while, because I'd never seen a modern commode. The whole room was a sight, with shiny mirrors and flowery walls and dried flowers in a bowl that smelled wonderful. In the outhouse at home I'd always had to hold my nose.

But finally the fascination wore off. And the next time the phone rang, I decided I had to answer it. I picked it up off its base and reached to press the button next to a flashing light. All I heard was a "Hello, is Be—?" and then nothing. When the phone rang again, I must have done the very same thing because for a second I heard a voice and then nothing—just a buzzing sound.

Anyway, when Becky got back, the phone was ringing again, and when she picked it up, I guess it was the person who I'd lost. When they were done talking, she let out a deep breath and came and stood in the doorway.

"The mail worked out fine." She folded one hand over the other, which seemed to be a habit of hers, and then straightened her hair. She looked ready to collapse from stress. Either that or explode. "I'll show you how to use the phone another time. You can just wash rocks for the rest of the day."

And that was what I ended up doing.

"Quitting time, Glory," Becky called to me from the front room. I figured maybe she was avoiding me. Maybe she didn't want to look me in the eye. Maybe she was feeling guilty because she was fixing to take my job away.

I stood up slowly and dusted myself off. I guess there'd been no point in wearing my best clothes. What wasn't covered by the apron Becky had given me was dirty and dusty, and I hadn't been in the fancy front room since I'd arrived.

I pulled my coat off the hanger next to Becky's, then pulled hers off, too. Reluctantly, nervously, I carried it out to her.

"Here you go," I said, putting it on the counter beside her. She was leaning over some figures, deep in thought. I just stood there, feeling I should say something. I'd already said "sorry" three dozen times.

"Do you think maybe you don't want to try me out anymore?" I muttered. "Because you can send me away if you want to. I'm sure I can do something else for money."

Yet another lie—I didn't know what I'd do without this work. Wrong or not, I was convinced there wasn't another soul in town who'd hire me.

Becky looked up from her figures. I felt like she was looking right into my brain as she froze for a few seconds. Then her face softened with sympathy.

"Everybody has a bad day," she said. "Yours just happened to be your first. I'll see you Thursday."

My heart leapt, but then immediately I felt all hot and cold inside. Maybe she felt sorry for me, and she was just being kind.

I needed that, but I didn't want it. I didn't want anybody's pity.

"Thanks, Becky," I forced myself to say. I'd promised myself to do anything to get to Boston, and if I had to accept charity, well, so be it. Then on second thought I added, "You won't be sorry."

She wouldn't be. I'd learn all there was to learn. And then I'd be the best worker she'd ever had. I knew I could do it.

I just didn't have the slightest idea how.

"Glory . . ."

I'd just been heading for the door. I turned now, nervous all over again.

"Did you take your lunch break today?"

I shook my head.

Becky cringed and rubbed her forehead. "Oh, gosh, I'm sorry, honey. You get an hour for lunch. I just assumed . . ." She trailed off. "Well, from now on."

Still mute, I nodded this time. And turned again to go. Becky's last words for the night followed me out:

"A girl as skinny as you should never go without a meal. You might shrivel up and blow away."

The days I didn't work went much slower. The minutes crawled by because I had not one thing that I could do.

Folks at home always said idleness was the devil's hand tool, and even though I didn't see how I could get in too much mischief in my present situation, I tried to keep myself busy. I rambled all over the woods near my clearing. I managed to gather a few bear-berries and walnuts and cook up a sort of compote over the fire. Each night I sat bundled up in Lincoln's backseat while I ate and kept my mind busy with thoughts of Boston.

Lincoln was like a sanctuary to me. Cold as it was in the woods, the nearby fire managed to keep the car warm and even cozy. When I wasn't too exhausted from work, I liked to lie in the back and watch the firelight dance along the walls. It made me feel good that I had taken this unloved car and made it a warm little home. I even talked to Lincoln sometimes when I felt too lonely and longed for the sound of my own voice.

I also spent many hours coming up with a list of things to do once I got to Boston. This meant sitting still for a long time and remembering talk after talk Katie and I, and sometimes her mama, had had about the city—to help me remember all the things Katie and I had wanted to do. It gave me a heartache, but I forced myself to concentrate all the same and eventually came up with this list:

The things I have to do in Boston:
Ride the swan boats
Eat in a restaurant with a real waiter
Read a newspaper all the way through
Go to the top floor of a skyscraper
Ride in a taxi
Be happy

I wasn't sure that last one was possible, and I almost didn't put it in there. But I decided it was important. It would have been important to Katie. I didn't think of how I'd pay for the other things or even how I would get by in Boston while I was doing them. But that was something I couldn't change right now. I'd have to cross that bridge when I got to it.

Saturday, Sunday, and Monday went almost as slowly as Wednesday and Friday had, though I did some more exploring on those days—around town, mostly. I even dropped into the store twice just to say hello to Becky. Blessedly, I didn't have any more coughing fits. And that was a good sign, I figured. At least it meant I had time. I hoped.

I desperately waited for Tuesday to come around again. When it did, I was overjoyed to return to the store.

Somewhere around eleven o'clock that day, Becky came into the back room. The door up front hadn't jingled for a while, and the sudden sound of her footsteps startled me. I had a mug of coffee in my hand, which I'd finally had the courage to ask for and was quite pleased I had—it was wonderful. Becky was holding a rectangular piece of plastic with two holes in the middle.

"It's time to get down to business," she said. I squinted at the object in her hands, wondering if this had something to do with how I'd be paid for my work. I'd been aching with curiosity about exactly how and when that would happen, but I was too afraid to ask and offend her somehow, after she'd been so nice to me.

She gazed out from under her eyebrows at me, a very serious look on her face. "If you're gonna work here, you're gonna have to be a fan." She lifted the piece of plastic and inserted it into a special part of the radio. Then she pressed a button, her lips curving up into a smile I couldn't read. And then there it was.

"... seas must the white dove sail, before she sleeps in the sand? ... How many ..."

Becky watched closely for my response. "You know Bob Dylan?"

I was tempted to nod, but instead I said honestly, "No."

Becky sighed. "I guess most people your age don't. But just listen. I think you'll like him."

She continued watching me, a smile playing about her lips as the man on the radio sang on, asking all these questions and then saying that the answers were blowing in the wind. I didn't understand it, really—how answers could be drifting around in the air— but still, it was very soulful, and mournful, and soft. I felt the smile on my face widen to mirror Becky's. It was so . . . *good.* It made me feel soothed and happy and sad all at the same time. I didn't even care that this had nothing to do with my getting paid.

Becky let out a laugh. "I knew it! I knew you'd be a fan!"

She gave me an amused, satisfied look.

"It's lovely," I said.

"Lovely," she repeated, and laughed. "My kids can't stand the stuff. My husband says I need to catch up to the rest of the world. I guess I should."

That makes two of us, I thought. But then I noticed Becky had stopped smiling. She was staring at me now, very seriously.

"Is something wrong?" I blurted out. Her look made me uneasy.

"You know, speaking of my family, I've been thinking about something." There was an awkward silence as I waited for her to finish.

"You know, you have a place to go if you need it, Glory," she said.

I swallowed my smile right there on the spot. What did she mean, a place to go? "What?" I asked. Suddenly I couldn't hear the music. And I couldn't look Becky in the eye. It was just that again, she seemed to know too much about me.

She put a hand on my shoulder.

"I'm not blind, honey."

Oh, God. Oh, God. Was this really happening? Then why was she being so calm? If she knew everything I'd told her was a lie?

"I see you come here in these clothes that don't fit, and I see you heading out of town on foot, and you came by twice Saturday looking chilled to the bone, and I just, well, since we first talked, I've kind of suspected that you don't have anyone *really* looking after you."

I was literally shaking now. What did she mean, "place to go"? Did that mean to the police? I couldn't face being caught. I couldn't.

"Hey, it's all right," Becky soothed, suddenly softening. She put both her hands on my shoulders now to still me. "Glory, I'm sorry I scared you!" Then her arms were around me and her perfume washed over me and I crumpled into her. But I didn't say a word. Finally she pulled back and leveled me with her glance.

"Look, honey, why don't you . . . well, why don't you talk it over with your mom? I know we've only known each other a few days, but if your mom's too sick to look out for you right now . . . I just . . . my kids would love you, and I think you're sweet as could be. And you could still go home as often as you wanted. . . ."

I couldn't grasp what she was trying to say. At least it seemed like she still believed my story, but if that was true, what was she getting at?

"But if you need to be taken in by somebody else for a while . . ." she continued. She was nervous, I could see, but she didn't look half as nervous as I was. I felt like all my organs had switched places and my heart was pounding in several spots at once—my head, my stomach, my throat. Then she said it. The thing I was least expecting to hear. And by her look, I could tell she meant it.

"Glory," she said. "What I mean is, you're welcome to come stay with me and my family."

In the silence that came after, all I could hear was the coffeepot, bubbling away.

CHAPTER
FIVE

"Would you mind grabbing that box, Glory?" Becky asked, her own arms full. "It goes in the back with the office supplies."

Nodding, I picked up the one she'd been pointing at and headed into the back, laying it down beside the desk. It was Friday morning, and I wasn't supposed to be here, but I was, doing whatever Becky needed me to do.

I hadn't taken her up on her offer. Not that it wasn't very, very tempting, because it would mean getting in out of the cold, and especially because it would mean spending more time with Becky (which would sure beat being alone). But for one thing, my folks brought me up not to take what I couldn't pay back. For the other thing, and maybe more importantly, it was hard enough keeping my secrets covered up at work. I couldn't imagine doing it every hour of the day. What about the schoolwork I was supposed to be doing? What about my "mama" who was supposed to be home sick?

So I refused Becky's offer, and I kept up with my lies. But I also started hanging around the store more—helping out even without being paid and dropping by whenever I knew Sara wasn't going to be around. I'd see her occasionally when I walked by the store on the afternoons she worked, but I didn't fancy crossing paths with her again, after what a fool I'd made of myself that first time and how ill-tempered she'd been.

By and by, though, I did get to learn more about Becky: her life, her children, where she grew up. She had lived in Shadow Tree since she was born. She was married to a man who drove trucks as his job and who was often away for weeks at a time. Her kids were six, thirteen, and fourteen years old. Their names were Andrew, and Bo, and Amelia, and they went to school not far from here. They rarely came into the store, Becky said, on account of her always managing to give them work to do.

But somehow, as I got to asking more and more questions about Becky, she seemed to ask fewer and fewer questions about me. At first she'd been curious about my mama, how she was doing and what she was sick with, and where the rest of my family was (my daddy, I told her, had run off years ago, and I had no brothers or sisters). She'd asked about my studies and my friends (I said I didn't have time for friends). But now she seemed to forget that I had any life outside of the store at all, and I was so busy, sometimes so did I.

Mainly this forgetting happened when I was making jewelry. When I'd finished polishing every rock I could find and done all the carrying and hauling and organizing that needed doing, she let me make a try at it. She showed me how to drill holes in the stones and match colors and how different beads and stones complemented each other. She showed me the different wires and how to knot them properly and the different clasps and hooks and how to attach them. And believe it or not, I turned out to be good at it.

"How's your mom doing?" Startled, I stopped my work. I hadn't heard Becky come into the back room.

My mind immediately went to Mama. How *was* she doing? Was she missing me still? Where was she right now? In the kitchen? Sitting on a chair by the fire, knitting? But as soon as I thought all this, I realized this wasn't what Becky was asking. I pictured an imaginary mama instead.

"Uh, she's doing . . . as well as you could expect."

Becky tilted her chin, her eyes shifting out of focus. "Good," she said. Then she turned and went back out front.

On my way out that evening I sank into a dismal mood. I dreaded the three-day break ahead, away from Becky and the warmth of the store. I gathered my coat and hat and mittens and scarf. Becky, who'd been sitting at the desk beside me, working, saw me bundling up to go and stopped me.

"Wait a sec." She finished whatever she was scribbling and then opened the desk drawer, pulled out an envelope, and handed it to me. It hadn't been licked and stuck. She motioned me to open it, so I did. Inside was a stack of money!

"I figured you'd want cash instead of a check."

"Thank you, Becky!" I felt all glowy inside. Money! Finally.

The old urgency rose up in me again just at the idea of being this much closer to getting my bus ticket.

"Well, gosh, now I feel really bad," Becky said. I squinted at her. "You look like you've won the lottery, sweetie. I wanted to pay you earlier—you know, payday's every two weeks— 'cause I figured you might need it. I didn't feel I could until these payments came in, though." She shrugged and gave me her typical sweet, almost pitying look. "I should've known you needed it more than me. I can just tell by the look on your face."

I assured Becky that I was just excited to get my first real pay, but didn't seem to put her at ease.

But by the time I'd made it three steps up Main Street, I'd forgotten about that. I stopped and frantically counted the bills in the envelope: One hundred and twenty dollars! I'd spent almost all of Jake's money on groceries, but another payday and I'd have more than enough—as long as I didn't get too sick before then. But the coughing fits had been blessedly rare since I started working for Becky.

Of course, while I planned to tuck every cent of my pay away in my little hidey-hole in Lincoln, there were a few things I'd just have to buy to get me through that time. Like more food.

But first I was gonna do something even better and just as necessary. I was gonna go get myself some warm clothes. Ones that actually fit.

*   *   *

If I'd been surprised at how much some things could cost out here in the modern world, I was truly flabbergasted at how cheap clothes could be.

The first few stores I poked my nose into on Saturday morning—the ones on Main Street—had made it seem the opposite. Everything was so expensive. I'd quickly given up on Main Street, but soon after I'd wandered farther out of the center of town, I found what I was looking for.

The way I knew it was the store for me was that it was called Hand-Me-Down Treasures, and Hand-Me-Down was a name I understood since that's mostly the kind of clothes I got in Dogwood (either hand-me-down clothes or new clothes made out of hand-me-down fabrics).

There were also a few different items in the windows—a bright red sweater, a crisscrossed red-and-pink skirt shaped like an A—and next to them, prices: $3.00, $4.00. Perfect.

The door didn't jangle, and nobody even gave me a second glance when I went in. All around there were clothes piled up in bins, clothes hanging from long silver poles, clothes on shelves. There were shoes for sale, and lots of doodads that didn't seem to be for much of anything, and even blankets. The whole place smelled like dust and also a little like the old folks I knew back home.

Taking my time because my money was precious, I drifted among the shelves, looking for just the right clothes. In the end I chose stuff like Becky's—two pairs of ribbed pants like hers, a couple of thick wool sweaters—because I didn't know enough to pick out anything much different.

But then there was the dress. It was deep blue, and it puckered in the back. It was prettier than anything I'd ever owned. *What are you doing? You hate dresses.* And I did. At least I always had, on account of all the women in town having to wear them. But even as I thought this, I pulled the dress off the rack. I knew I shouldn't spend the money (it was only four dollars and fifty cents, but money was money). Still, I couldn't make my fingers let it go. And would four dollars and fifty cents really keep me from getting to Boston in time? No. Especially now that everything was going so well.

I picked up a soft, puffy blanket after that and two matching rose-patterned sheets (they were only fifty cents each) to cover Lincoln's seats with and make it extra cozy. And some long underwear and some regular.

As the lady typed away the numbers at the register, I itched to get back to the ridge and fix up Lincoln's seats. And make my bed. And try on my new dress.

New dress.

I'd make a modern girl of myself yet.

I picked up jewelry making like I'd been born doing it. Which was surprising, considering how bad I'd always been at sewing and indoor work and how impatient I usually was.

But making jewelry was different. I loved figuring out what colors would look pretty together and thinking about the person who would buy it and how pretty they'd feel wearing it. And I know it sounds foolish, but the best part was that each kind of stone gave off a different mood. Turquoise felt like summer. Onyx felt mysterious, like a lady dressed in a long dark dress. And I used these feelings to pick the kind of jewelry I made—fancy or simple or flashy or quiet.

Becky said I was gifted, and when she did, I almost fell off my stool. I'd been called sharp, even clever, but all my life I'd always heard that more than anything else, I was useless. People'd always called it lazy, but the way I figured, it was the exact opposite. I was just too restless to sit and work at something for too long.

But making jewelry—my own designs, not the patterned stuff—was something I could do for hours and hours and not even blink an eye. It never got boring because it made me use my brain. And according to Becky, I had a "creative" brain. Which sounded like a compliment, even though *creative* was a word folks didn't use in Dogwood and probably would have used as a scold if they had. She even said she'd let me start on the expensive stones soon. Of course, I didn't think I'd be around that long. But when I said this to Becky, she just waggled her hand in the air as if to say, "I guess."

It was the socializing that was hard. Becky started introducing me to customers now and then and even had me working out front at the counter (making jewelry there in the downtime) more and more often, especially when she'd have to take a call from her husband or one of her kids in private.

Folks were nice, mostly, and I was grateful for that. Becky seemed to know everyone, and it was like they accepted me because they accepted her. But every time I'd have to talk to someone new, my stomach would clench up. One of these days, I feared, a police person of some sort would walk through that door. Or at least some stranger who'd get suspicious and tell the police. But amazingly, nobody did. And I got to worrying less and less.

And it's just as well because when disaster came, it had nothing to do with the police or with socializing.

The Thursday of my third week, Becky got a call. She came into the back room, her forehead scrunched up with worry as she pulled her hair back into a bun and knotted it tightly.

"Glory, Amelia's broken her ankle at cheerleading. I gotta run over to the school and pick her up. Can you close for me?"

I nodded, feeling panicked.

"You can just close up early. Lock the doors. Lock the register and turn out the lights. We won't bother setting the alarm—I'm worried it might go off by accident."

Becky had pulled on her coat and was yanking her hat down over her forehead.

"Don't look so scared, honey. You'll be fine."

"Don't worry, Becky, I can do it." I took the keys she held out to me and tried a reassuring smile.

In another minute she was gone. I wished I'd said something about hoping her daughter was okay. I wished I had a mother to worry about me if I ever broke an ankle or something like that. I envied Becky's daughter. A spiteful part of me even disliked her for being so lucky, for having a family that wanted her and a mother as wonderful as Becky.

Sighing, I headed straight to the door and put up the CLOSED sign, scared of getting customers while I was here alone. Then I set about turning off lights, as I'd seen Becky do, and tidying up in the back. It was eerie, being here by myself. I headed out front to lock the register.

I'd watched Becky use this contraption, in fascination, many times—tapping away at the numbers and symbols. The little buttons were glistening and winking at me. I never could resist fiddling with a knob or a clasp back home, and now those buttons were too tempting to ignore. I leaned in and pushed one after another, little clicking sounds coming out with each push. Then I guess I pushed a button for the money drawer because it came shooting out of its slot with a clatter.

Its contents were mesmerizing. Bills of all sorts sat stacked inside—tens and twenties and even one fifty. I did the math in my head. There was more than two hundred dollars in here. Enough to get me to Boston tomorrow. Added to the money I had back in Lincoln, it was more than enough.

Musing on this, I moved my fingers over the bills, feeling their surfaces, wondering at how these little bits of paper could do so much. I simply needed to . . .

Glory!

With great force I slammed the drawer shut and locked it. My breathing was heavy and fast. Never, ever, *ever* would I resort to stealing. Especially not from Becky. Without another thought I grabbed my coat, my hat and mittens and scarf, turned off the rest of the lights, and headed out the front door, locking it behind me.

The streets had emptied out for the day, and the street-lights—still beautiful and stunning to me—reflected off the puddles of melted snow in the road. I longed to be curled up under my covers already, cozy in Lincoln's backseat.

Feeling satisfied that I'd made it out of temptation's way, relief washed over me. In fact, I felt a little proud of myself. *There, God, you see?* I thought as I made my way out of town. *I'm an honest person. Don't you think you could help me? Don't you think you could get me to Boston in one piece, alive and well enough to do those things I need to do for Katie?*

I hoped that God heard me. I hoped He was watching and

regretting all He'd let happen to me. I hoped He was looking down at me, like He'd looked down at Job, and thinking what a good person I was and figuring on making it all up to me somehow.

Before I even made it to the clearing, I sensed something was wrong. The trees seemed extra quiet. And somehow less peaceful—like every creature was holding its breath.

I knew. Somehow I knew what had happened. I broke into a run before I was out of the trees. Suddenly my own stupidity was as clear as day. To fix up the car with curtains and all, so near the road and the town, for anyone who came along to see and . . .

Please please please, no.

It was that first sight of Lincoln that made me pull up short. All four doors were open. The sheets and the blankets had been pulled out and were lying in dirty piles beside the car.

No. In another second I was in a mad dash. I leapt into the front seat, digging in the hidey-hole, my heart thumping.

Nothing.

They'd taken all of it. Somebody had come here, and found the money I'd saved so carefully, and taken it. I dropped my face into my right hand, digging at my forehead with my fingertips. *It's okay, it's okay,* I told myself. *Breathe.*

Snapping up my head again, I now took in the shambles of the car itself. The seats I'd scrubbed and polished were torn and caked with mud. Two back windows had been smashed. There was nothing here to show that for the last few weeks, this had been my home—that it had meant more to someone than just a piece of garbage.

Then I had another thought, and my breath caught in my throat, and my insides caught fire. *Please, no.*

My photograph. It wasn't on the ledge where I'd left it, next to Jake's note, which was still there. It wasn't on the floor. I pulled apart the blankets, but nothing. I tumbled out of the car and crawled around the ground. No. It was gone. Gone, gone, gone.

I groaned, throwing my head back and rising to my feet. Then my body just took over. My legs started kicking the car. My fists started pounding. And I didn't know if the screaming was in my head or coming out of my mouth. Finally I collapsed onto the wet, snowy, muddy ground, cross-legged. And the tears started to come.

All the money Jake had given me. And all the money I'd saved. All my food. Lincoln.

And my picture. Why had they taken my picture?

My tears turned into harsh, dry coughing fits. Between every breath I looked about the ground with blind hope.

It seemed like I was going to cry forever. Minutes passed, I don't know how many, and the tears kept coming out. I wiped at my eyes with my sleeve. Once. Twice. I looked around again, as if for help. But I knew there was no help.

And then there it was.

I thought I was imagining it, so I wiped at my eyes again. Then I scrambled over on my knees. I yanked it out of the mud, and when I saw that it was my photograph after all, I gasped with relief. It was soggy and ripped, and it had a muddy boot print on it, but it was still here.

Leaning back against Lincoln, I clutched it to my chest, crying even harder. This picture was all I had left of my family, my old life, my real home. Even Boston didn't mean as much to me at this moment.

Eventually, after sitting in the mud for what seemed like hours, wondering what I was going to do—without any money at all, not even the forty dollars I'd started with—I felt my eyes dry. I crawled into Lincoln's empty, shredded backseat, pulling the dirty bedclothes in behind me. I wrapped myself in a ball amongst the mess and fell into a deep sleep.

I kept ahold of the picture the whole night through.

CHAPTER
SIX

Becky steered the car onto a narrow, windy road, and I couldn't speak for gazing out the window. The hills along both sides of the road rolled under snow. Houses and barns dotted them here and there, giving off smoke and standing out against the dusky sky. As we took curve after curve, I felt like I was going to be sick to my stomach—a feeling I was getting used to these days.

"It's not far," Becky reassured me, patting my leg. "Bo runs it sometimes. He's on the track team." She smiled with pride, as if I understood what a track team was or knew that it was something to be proud of.

I knew this was what I needed. I couldn't spend another day in the woods feeling cold and unsafe, on top of being penniless. And Becky had been more than happy when I'd asked her if I could still take her up on her offer. But it meant more strangers, and taking one step farther into a world I didn't belong in, and working that much harder to keep my secrets. I didn't want to meet her kids. I didn't want to meet anybody. I feared they'd dislike me or, worse, try to make friends. And I didn't want any new friends. All I wanted was to get to Boston.

I felt the bile rise up in my throat. That goal seemed as far away as ever, even though I'd already come miles and miles. Without the money I'd saved, it might as well be next to China. I hated whoever had stolen it. I knew that wasn't right, but I did.

"Now, don't you worry, Glory, the kids will love you," Becky said, misreading my worries. "They will." She tapped me on the knee for emphasis. "Amelia is beside herself, she's so thrilled to have a new roommate."

Amelia. Another instance of me having feelings that weren't right. Already I didn't like her, and I'd never even met her. It was something about her being my age and having so much while I had so little. And then, I'd never known a girl my age except Katie. I didn't want to know another girl besides Katie. Secretly I hoped Amelia'd be mean and disagreeable so I wouldn't feel bad for disliking her.

"Nick won't be home from his route till the eighth," Becky continued. "But he'll love you, too, when he gets here." Again, it didn't help. If I was intimidated by Becky's kids, I was even more intimidated by the thought of her husband. He'd be harder to lie to, for one. I doubted he could possibly be as accepting of my explanations as Becky.

Becky turned onto a street that, to my surprise, was lined with small houses that looked like they'd been cut out of the same mold and then just painted differently—with windows in all the same spots and flaky sidings that looked like the roof shingles back home. Her house was the third on the right.

My legs felt like jam as I stepped out of the car and slammed the door behind me. We were about halfway up the walk when the front door flew open.

Standing there, outlined in the yellow light pouring from inside, was a very pretty girl with rosy cheeks and deep dimples. She was holding onto the wall with one hand, her left foot lifted gingerly into the air and covered in plaster. She was as blond as the day is long, and her eyes twinkled with an expression of amusement as she looked at me.

Becky cleared her throat. "Your manners, Miss Amelia."

Amelia's white teeth beamed through in a smile. "Come on in," she said. Behind her I could see two boys standing near the sofa, staring. Becky walked into the room first, I followed, and Amelia hopped on behind us.

"Glory, this is Bo and Andrew. And of course, Amelia. My kids are very excited about having a houseguest. I hope they don't maul you." I could tell Becky said this for their benefit as well as mine because she looked at them when she said it. "Have a seat," she added to me. Then she disappeared down the hall that went off to the right. Her voice echoed from whatever room she was in. "Tacos okay for dinner?" she asked.

"Yes, thank you," I answered politely, since nobody else did. Of course, I'd never heard of tacos.

Stiffly I put my knapsack down and sat on the nearest chair, folding my hands and sitting up straight. To my surprise, Amelia lowered herself right beside me onto the arm, flipping her ponytail. I scooted sideways.

"You're gonna be my roommate," she gushed, while I shrank away. "It's gonna be great. I've always wanted a roommate. It'll be like having a sister."

"Glory, I'm gonna go ahead and start cooking," Becky called as she came back down the hall. "Make yourself at home." Then she disappeared into another doorway closer to where we were sitting, and the sound of pots and pans banging around followed.

"Yeah, great," the oldest boy, Bo, piped in, both of them seeming not to have heard Becky. "Like we need another girl to take up the bathroom all the time."

"Don't be rude." Amelia leaned over and punched him on the arm, then turned back to me, an apology in her eyes. "Ignore him. He's probably just trying to get your attention. Anyway, I'm just excited, that's all."

Bo let out a snort as he retreated toward the stairs. There was a set that went down and another that went up. Bo headed downstairs. I just squeezed my hands together tighter till the tips of my fingers turned red.

All this time, while I sat speechless, little Andrew had been standing stock-still in front of me. His feet were together, his arms down at his sides, and his big brown eyes trained solemnly on my face. Now a whole bundle of questions came tumbling out of his mouth, and he started gesturing and blinking rapidly. "How old are you?" "Do you have a dog?" "Will you have to baby-sit me?" "Do you like soccer?" "What about alligators?"

Before I could say a word, he began to answer the questions as if they'd been directed at himself. "I want a dog, but Mom won't let me have one because she's allergic. But once we went to the zoo and saw alligators, and they're better than dogs, anyway, and they're my favorite animal because—"

"Kids! Stop treating Glory like she's the circus just come to town," came Becky's voice from what I figured was the kitchen, down the hall. I wished I could be in there with her instead of out here feeling nervous and shy and confused. "Andy, go on upstairs and do something useful like cleaning your room, which I'm *sure* could use it. Amelia, please show Glory around."

Andrew was standing with his face very close to mine. But as he heard Becky's voice, his eyes widened, and then he was off like a flash to the stairs. Only he went down, like Bo had, not up. I would've smiled if I wasn't so jittery—he was a "character." That's what my mama would have said.

Amelia, sweet as pie, leaned toward me with a grin and squeezed my elbow. "You want the grand tour?"

"Um, okay," I replied, pulling out of her grasp and standing up.

In a flash she had hopped across the room and grabbed a

pair of crutches, like the ones old Mr. White with the clubfoot had back home, only fancier. After resting one under each armpit, she motioned me forward. Unfortunately we walked right past the kitchen. I longed for Becky's protection.

The short hall leading off the common room where we'd been sitting was bordered by three other rooms: the kitchen, a bathroom (all in blue and even nicer than the one at the store), and some kind of sitting room. Upstairs was another bathroom and bedrooms. One, Amelia pointed out, was her parents', with fluffy lavender-colored blankets and matching curtains and a man's jacket hanging in the corner that must have belonged to Becky's husband.

Amelia's room was next, but she only cracked the door open for a second to drop off my knapsack and my coat and hat. "We'll save *that* till later," she said.

"Bo's room." She opened this door quickly, as if there couldn't be a more boring sight. Only long enough for me to see a pile of clothing and a bed covered in unmade gray—gray blanket, sheet, pillow. How come everything matched so well? And how could someone—a boy at that—have so much clothing? Becky and her husband, I guessed, must have a lot of money.

Andrew's room, which was next, was equally crowded with clothes and God knew what else. He seemed to have a lot of toys—but not the wooden kind we had in Dogwood. They were brightly colored, and shiny plastic, and shaped like cars

and miniature people. I just gawked, not quite able to comprehend that all this *stuff* belonged to only a few children. And
then . . . all the rooms, I was noticing, and the halls, too, were
covered in a rug that went from one wall to the other, leaving
not a speck of floor uncovered. My feet sank right into it, leaving soft prints behind me.

Finally we went back downstairs, and then down the other
flight, and Amelia hopped ahead of me into a big, messy space
with a large glass door on one side. The boys were here, gathered in front of what I knew right away must be a television
set. *A television set.*

On the glass square before us, two men were locked in a
fight. Each had his arms wrapped about the other and they were
rolling around on the ground. My hands flew up to my mouth.

"You're not allowed to be watching this," Amelia said, missing my reaction altogether. She walked up to the set and
pushed a few buttons. Different, amazing moving images flick-
ered by, till finally Amelia rested on one that just had two
women talking. They, too, seemed to be arguing, but at least
they weren't punching each other. I sighed in relief.

Finally Amelia seemed to notice my openmouthed stare.

"Don't you like soaps, Glory?"

"What?" I asked, knocked out of my daze. "Oh, no. Um,
we don't have a television at home. Yet." I added that last part
in hindsight, just to sound more normal.

"You don't have a TV?!" Andrew asked, right before Amelia shot him an angry look.

"Some people can't afford TVs, Andy. Remember, Mom explained to us?" She glanced at me quickly.

"But you haven't even—?"

"Hush," Amelia replied.

Andrew's lips shut tight, but his eyes were still wide with surprise. Bo ignored us altogether, slumping deeper into his seat.

Amelia just stood there, blushing. I could feel myself blushing, too. I wondered what Becky had told them about me, especially about me not being able to afford things. What kind of a person did they think I was? Did they feel sorry for me? But I couldn't tear my attention away from the television for long enough to worry too much. Even my nervousness had disappeared for the moment.

"Well, then, do you wanna watch this, Glory?" Amelia asked, shifting her crutches out from under her armpits and seeming disappointed. "I guess it might be a treat for you."

"Yes, please," I said, mesmerized and not even looking at her.

Andrew scooted over, and I gingerly sat next to him.

You see, Lorraine, one woman on the television said, her face bunched up in a snarl, *I know you weren't with Kyle last night.* At those words, some music started playing and the other woman, Lorraine, I guessed, got a very scared look on her face that lasted forever—she didn't move a muscle. I thrust the nails of my right hand into my mouth and nibbled. Why was where she had been so important? Wherever it was, it seemed she was about to get in a barrel of trouble.

A million questions on top of this one spun through my head. How was television possible? Were these women really fighting, or was it pretend? Where did all these pictures come from, and how did they get into the television box in front of us? But I knew I couldn't ask a one of them without looking backward in front of these modern kids.

I was still watching when Becky called downstairs to say that dinner was ready. I don't think I blinked the entire time.

The tacos were divine. I helped myself to five and didn't realize how much that was till I looked up and saw both boys and Amelia staring at me in astonishment.

"You did a fine job with these tacos," I blurted through a mouthful of food, by way of explaining my appetite. Which for some reason made the whole table, minus Becky, burst into laughter. I felt myself blush.

We were seated at a round, glass-topped table in the kitchen, which was by far my favorite room in the house. It was filled with gadgets and covered from wall to wall in yellow— yellow walls, shiny yellow floor, and a window with yellow-and-white-striped curtains.

"Thank you, Glory," Becky said, casting a death look to her kids. My mama would have just yelled at me for my rudeness, talking with my mouth full, but Becky didn't seem to mind. "Nick's not big on tacos, so it's a special treat for when he's away."

After we were done eating, I tried to help Becky wash up, but she wouldn't hear of it. So I set a course straight for the television, which was where I was desperate to be. But before I got a foot onto the stairs, I felt a hand on my back, and with a sinking heart, I turned to see Amelia flashing her dimples at me.

"Come on upstairs—I'll show you my stuff," she said, taking me by the arm with one free hand and holding on to one crutch with the other. I marveled at her confidence. I marveled even more at her nerve. What made her so sure I wanted to see her "stuff" or wanted to be friends at all?

Her confidence, though, wasn't half so much of a marvel as her room. She closed the door behind us as I took it all in—the bedcover, decorated with tiny brown flowers curving through a deep red background; the walls with a trim of flowers along the top to match. A picture of a man holding some kind of banjo-type thing in his arms hung behind the bed.

"Are you an artist?" I breathed, wondering how she could have gotten such intricate flowers painted up there—and forgetting for a moment to keep Amelia at arm's length. The closest we had to anything like an artist in Dogwood was my grandpa, who used to be able to whittle anything in the world out of a plain piece of wood—a miniature black bear, a duck, a flute. But Mrs. Johansen had loved art of all sorts. She'd said that artists blessed the world by showing it to itself in little glimpses. I sure missed her way of putting things, though I doubted she ever missed me. *Rued the day I was born was more like it,* I thought sadly.

Amelia just shook her head, though, looking at me blankly. "Nah. I'm more into science," she said, leaning her crutch beside her bed and plopping down onto the covers. "Not so much into art. My dad says I should go into law, though, the way I talk so much, and . . ."

I was disappointed. As she went on talking, I tried to listen politely and survey the room at the same time. A desk stood against one wall with a mirror behind it, and a kind of scarf made out of pale red feathers draped over its seat. Between it and the bed were shelves upon shelves with all sorts of things piled on them in disarray: books, miniature horses of all sizes and colors, little flat, square boxes with pictures on them—there were at least twenty of those, and I wondered what they were for. This is what Mrs. White would have called spoiled as a rotten egg. So many things for just one girl.

Following my gaze, Amelia plucked one of the squares from the shelf. "Do you have any CDs?" she asked. I shook my head as she hobbled over to a radio—her own radio!—and pushed a button that made the top pop up. She took a round disc out of the square case and plunked it into the slot. Pretty soon there was music coming out. I marveled at all the ways you could play music without an instrument in sight.

"Mom said you might not have that kind of stuff." Amelia patted a spot beside her on the bed.

I sat, but I bristled at the comment, wondering if she meant it as an insult. And I wondered how much more Becky had gleaned about me without my knowing.

"Oh, don't be embarrassed." Amelia covered my hand with her own and gave it a squeeze. I wanted to pull away, but instead I looked down at the two hands together. How white my skin looked next to hers! In the places where my hand poked out from underneath hers, I could see the veins blue as sapphires. "My mom's a die-hard hippie, anyway. We wouldn't even have a TV if it weren't for Dad. He likes football. And he says Mom just better accept that TV is a part of life. Mom said she thinks that's fine—if the TV is so much a part of his life, he can run off and marry it for all she cares." Amelia smiled.

"What's *your* mom like, if you don't mind my asking?" she said, suddenly turning serious.

I *did* mind. I minded talking about myself, period. I wished she would just mind her own business. But I couldn't say that.

I thought about my mama. I could see her standing in the church the night I was cast out—her hair pulled back in a bun, her dress tidy and modest, grief etched in every line of her face. I thought about how she'd fainted dead away, right before I drank from the vial of judgment, and I felt myself wince. Then I thought back further, to happier times, to her puttering around the house, carrying baby Marie in one arm and shuffling pots on the stove with the other. She was always doing three things at once.

"My mama's real nice," I said truthfully. Then, seeing that Amelia was waiting for more, I continued. "She sews a lot. She can make anything. Quilts and clothes and things." That went for most of the grown women in Dogwood, but my mama had had a real knack. I'd never appreciated it till just now. My mind sifted through visions of her laughing and even relaxing a time or two—though those times had been few and far between.

"She works really hard," I added, embarrassed to hear my voice cracking.

"I'm sorry she's not feeling well," Amelia said, fidgeting, her hand again moving softly to squeeze mine. "I've never had anyone I love get really sick. I'm sure it's terrible."

I just shrugged. And let my chin fall. I wondered if it was bad luck to tell everyone somebody was sick when they weren't. Even if it *was* for a good cause. But then maybe pretending I *wasn't* sick, when I actually was, evened everything out.

Amelia seemed like she wanted to say more. She looked at me very closely, started a few times, and stopped, then finally she asked, "You . . . you didn't catch it, did you?"

I didn't mean to, but I jolted at the question.

"I . . . I'm sorry. I just . . ."

"Do I look sick?" I asked. Was it so easy to see, even for a stranger? Maybe I had less time left than I thought.

"Oh. Oh, no," she sputtered. "It's just, you're, um, pale. But I guess it's just your skin tone." Amelia laughed nervously, and I didn't say a word. "Can you believe some of the girls in school go tanning in the winter? I mean, my mom would *kill* me. You look much healthier than them. Hey, I'll show you some pictures." She yanked a giant book out of her desk drawer, changing the subject fast.

But she'd lost me. I was already miles away.

Becky came in a while later and pulled out a bed she called a trundle that was hidden right under Amelia's own bed. I watched as she kissed Amelia good night, remarking how little alike they looked, thinking with a pang how unfair it was that Amelia should have her mama here every night and I should never see my own again. I envied that kiss—though only a kiss from my own mama would have pleased me.

I watched them awkwardly, feeling like an intruder, yet wishing for a good-night kiss of my own. Then Becky stood up, gave me a little wink, and, before disappearing through the door, told Amelia not to keep me up with her jabbering.

But that was exactly what Amelia did.

She talked about girls at her school—it seemed there must have been a hundred of them—and a few of the boys she liked. She showed me more photographs, of everything from her daddy (who was almost as big and burly as my own daddy, only much fairer) to her first birthday party to her schoolmates to her favorite horse at their neighbors' farm. I'd never seen such a collection of pictures before—Mrs. Johansen didn't have half so many.

"I wish you could go to school with me. You're lucky, though. It can be a pain sometimes." Amelia tilted her head to the side. "What's it like being home schooled? Mom said your mom is, like, your teacher, kind of. . . ."

"Kind of," I said, thinking back to the talk Becky and I had had about my moving into the Aiden house. I'd told her that I would still visit "home" on a few of the days when I wasn't working to see my mama and also to do my "schoolwork." She'd fallen over herself trying to get me to let *her* help with my schoolwork instead, but I'd refused. I hadn't the slightest idea what I'd really be doing on these days, but it seemed the only way to make things appear normal.

"It's good," I said now to Amelia. "But it's lonely." I was thinking of the days by myself.

Amelia continued to show me pictures. There were photographs of the school itself (which was too big to be believed) and Becky and Mr. Aiden. To my astonishment, there was even a picture of Jake, who I'd forgotten would have to be Amelia's cousin. He was a couple of years younger, but there was no mistaking his freckles and his dirty blond hair. I missed him.

The pictures were interesting, even amazing, but when Amelia launched into another story about a girl, Alicia, in one of the shots, I decided I couldn't listen a minute longer—even out of politeness.

I let my eyes flutter closed, making it look like I was trying my best to stay awake but that I was too sleepy. Katie would have seen through it in a heartbeat. But Amelia must have believed I really was sleepy because she finally quieted and turned out the light.

For the first time all day I had time to relax. But I couldn't, for all the thoughts going through my head. Many of them were about the girl lying next to me.

It wasn't that Amelia was disagreeable. She was much more agreeable than I would have liked—even if she *was* a bit of a babbler. But the fact was, her life was as different from mine as night and day. She had her whole life ahead of her, filled with excitement and socializing and boys—things I'd never experience. I knew I had less than a year ahead, filled with one thing and one thing only—getting to Boston.

I rolled onto my back and stared at the ceiling. There was a thin line of light slicing into the bedroom from the door and falling across the bed. It made me remember how the very same thing used to happen in my room back home. This room was warmer and more comfortable. The bed was soft. My bed back home had been so old that the middle of the mattress sank halfway to the floor when you got into it. But this bed wasn't home. And even though I was lucky to be here instead of out in the woods, I couldn't help thinking that made it not half as good.

Amelia wasn't Katie, either. There was only one place in my heart for a best friend. Even though Katie was dead, she still had that spot, and I didn't want anybody else trying to take it. I resented it, actually.

Anyway, I figured Amelia—the whole Aiden family, in fact— wouldn't be so eager to welcome me if they knew what I'd done to Katie and to everyone back home by taking Katie away from them. Mrs. Johansen loomed big in my mind. What I'd done to her was almost as bad as what I'd done to her daughter. I'd broken her heart. And broken my own mama's heart as well when she had to watch my poor daddy be the one to pass judgment on me. That night at the lake, I'd cost two women their daughters.

I hurt everyone who matters to me. It was the biggest reason why I'd do better not to care too much about this family, no matter how they tried to make me feel welcome.

CHAPTER
SEVEN

At first I took walks. Outside of the days I was supposed to be with my "mama"—when I would wander around town on my own—it was my time to quiet my head when the Aiden household got too overwhelming. I'd walk up and down their street many evenings at dusk. As the electric lights popped on here and there, I'd try to get a glimpse through the windows of house after house, wondering what kind of lives people were leading inside. It made me forget some of my nervousness.

When I returned to the house, Becky would look concerned—and mention that I should be careful of cars at this hour. But she seemed to sense that it did me good and never forbade me to go—as long as I made it back for dinner.

I also liked to retreat to the bathroom to take showers (which were amazing) and sometimes baths. Even just soaking in the Aidens' bathtub, with some of Amelia's fancy bath gel squirted in to make bubbles, was a whole different experience than bathing back home. I'd never felt so clean and warm and soft; I'd never smelled so good. And it was another time to be alone.

It was a lot of pressure, living with the Aidens. A lot of

being on my guard. Even the store was much better; at least there I'd get some time to myself at the worktable.

At the house there was always Amelia wanting to share some gossip about school or asking me too much about my history. A lot of times it was all I could do just to be polite, and sometimes I didn't even manage that. A time or two I pretended I didn't hear her or replied with an answer that was obviously meant to stop the conversation. Oblivious as she appeared to be, Amelia was no half-wit. Once or twice she seemed to pick up on my feelings and back away. But the next day she'd be at it again—with the same big smile and the usual friendly chatter.

Bo, on the other hand, pretty much ignored me after that first day. And that was its own sort of worrisome. It made me wonder if he hated having me here and if I was the reason he'd spend hours in front of the television, as if avoiding everyone. But Becky said he was just going through "his sulky phase," whatever that meant, and boys his age were just like that. I thought of my own brother, Theo—trying to remember what he was like when he was Bo's age. But it was different for him. Young people in Dogwood had too much work to have time to sulk.

Andrew was a whole different story. He was a kind little soul. True to our first meeting, he was as friendly as could be. He soon developed the habit of slipping his hand into mine when we watched television and sitting on my lap from time to time. Unlike Amelia, his friendliness didn't make me feel skittish or bitter. Unlike Bo, he didn't make me feel unwelcome.

Still, around any of the Aiden children I was always—always—scared of saying the wrong thing. Which I did *a lot.* Time after time, I'd ask a dumb question or give an answer about my past that didn't quite add up, and then I'd have to fret about it the rest of the day and wonder what the Aidens would do if they found out everything I'd told them was a big lie.

It's funny, though, how quickly something can start to seem normal. I guess even when you're seeing new and amazing things every day, seeing new and amazing things becomes normal. And that's the way it was in Shadow Tree. I got used to it quickly—even though the nervousness never left.

On days when I wasn't working, I found things to occupy myself downtown. My favorite was the library, where you could look at any books you wanted and it didn't cost anything. At first I'd thought it was too good to be true, and I'd been very shy about going inside. But soon it was a regular habit. It was wonderful to have a pick of so many books. The most we'd ever been allowed to read back home were a very few "classic moral tales," as the Reverend called them: *Pilgrim's Progress, Paradise Lost,* and the official history of our town. And I'd read all those as soon as I was old enough to struggle through them.

But the library was full of books on every subject, from adventure to romance to history. The one I really fell in love with was a story called *Gone With the Wind.* I'd picked it up because a quotation on the back had said it was "a monumental epic of the South," which made it sound like I might learn something about history from it. And I did. But when it turned out to be so much more, I was thrilled. It was like a thunderstorm—gusty and breathtaking and heartbreaking. I adored the main character, Scarlett O'Hara, from the first few pages and couldn't put the book down.

On top of all this, being at the library made me feel a little less dishonest. I was studying, sort of, like I'd told Becky. I was sort of schooling myself.

Rebecca's children had Saturday and Sunday to do what they pleased. They called it the weekend, and they didn't even go to church. I wondered if the Aidens were Christians at all, what with no Bible that I could see in the house and no saying grace before supper, but I didn't feel right asking.

Still, the second Sunday morning, at the last minute, Becky seemed to get the idea in her head that I might "be religious." And when she asked if I wanted her to take me to church, I surprised myself by saying yes.

She drove me and Andrew, who insisted on coming (as he often did now whenever I was headed anywhere), to the front door of a church not a five-minute drive away and promised to wait outside for us.

"I'm not much into church, honey, but you go ahead."

It struck me as such a strange thing to say. Imagine, if all those times Daddy or Teresa or Mama had dragged me out the door to worship, I'd just been able to say, "I'm not much into church. You go ahead without me."

Andrew and I approached the main doors as folks trickled inside. I remembered the last time I'd been in church. It was the last time I'd ever seen my family.

Chills ran up and down my skin as I pushed open the doors and we walked inside, but what lay before us was so different, so unfamiliar, that the chills quickly went away. We ducked into the first empty bench and stared about.

The church was enormous compared to the one at home. The benches were large enough to fit ten people each at least, but the whole room was only about half full. Andrew, who'd never been here either, squeezed my hand. It made me feel good, but I wished he hadn't come. I would rather have been alone.

Eventually a hush fell over the crowd, and everybody turned to look as a man—the reverend, I guessed—made his way up the center aisle. He was adorned in fancy white robes with a gold cross up front, and there were two boys behind him dressed the same. The boys were waving these little gold balls in front of them. And they were chanting something low and soft.

My Lord, it was the oddest thing I had ever seen!

Finally they reached the front of the room, and everybody stood up. Andrew and I followed along. Then the reverend started speaking. And then we had to sit down again. Stand up. Sit down. Stand up. Finally we settled into our seats for good as the reverend started talking about loaves and fishes—which was at least one thing I was familiar with. But for all the fanciness, it was as hard to concentrate on him as it had been to concentrate on Reverend Clifton during worship back home.

I tried and tried to understand the message, but it didn't take long for my mind to start drifting. I couldn't do it. Still, I figured I'd taken the trouble to come, and I might as well use the time wisely. Andrew looked to be half asleep, so I let go of his hand and clasped mine both together.

Strange as it may seem, I was nervous as I started to pray. I'd been so mad at God for so long, and I knew that was sinful. I wondered if He was sore with me right back and realized He must be. Part of me didn't even want to bother to make it up. But part of me knew I should at least try.

God, I said in my mind, *look, I came to church and I didn't even have to. Maybe you could send me a sign to say you know I'm here?*

I looked around the church and waited. And waited. Nothing.

Okay, I continued in my head. *Well, I just wanted to thank you for sending me to the Aidens. I mean, getting me robbed was a dirty trick, especially after I was so good about the money in the drawer, but . . .*

I stopped myself. No sense scolding God. I tried again. *You can't blame me for not being too happy with you right now. But maybe if you'd just send me some sign. To let me know you're still looking out for me. To let me know that maybe I'm not gonna go to hell and that I'm gonna make it to Boston and that you still care about what happens to me.*

I waited, but again, nothing. The preacher droned on in a monotone, which I had to own was much nicer than the Reverend's screeching and hollering. The folks in the other benches were listening patiently.

Nothing changed. I had the eerie feeling that I was praying to the air. That God wasn't even listening.

Where are you? I asked inside. But God must not have heard. There was no reply. There'd never been a reply.

Andrew was now fully asleep beside me. I gently took his hand and shook him awake, and when his eyes fluttered open, I led him out of the aisle.

Becky was waiting in the lot to the side of the building, leaned back in her car, reading. When she saw me, she sat up in surprise.

"That was short. What happened?"

I looked back over my shoulder, as if to find an answer for her there. It was too much to say. I never wanted to be in a church again. God had abandoned me, *if* He was up there at all. Which didn't seem so sure anymore.

"I changed my mind," was all I said. And without another word I got in the car.

That night the coughing came back. Like before, it was loud and harsh and it took my breath away. Lucky for me, I was on one of my walks, and nobody saw.

*   *   *

"You sure you can cook?" Becky asked, looking at me skeptically. I gave her my most convincing expression, coupled with my most convincing nod, and it seemed to do the trick. I'd always been an okay cook, but I'd never really tried to do it alone. Surely if I put my mind to it, I'd do fine.

We'd just gotten back from the grocery store. Not Pete's. A much bigger grocery store called Food King, with wide, glowing aisles of food under long white lights, doors that opened and closed without even being touched—Becky said the doors could actually *sense* us walking toward them, if you can believe that—and countertops that moved all on their own near the cash registers. There was soft music everywhere and more food than even a king could ever want.

I'd carefully picked out a few items to buy for myself—some vitamin pills (maybe they'd help with the coughing) and a bar of chocolate (I couldn't resist). It was only when Becky and I were at the register, and I was watching her pay for her purchases, that I even thought about real food. The little sign above the cash register flashed a number, $134. And I realized how much it must be costing the Aidens to feed and take care of me.

On the way home Becky'd refused my offer to give her money for my keep. But, resolved not to live on her charity, I'd insisted on doing chores around the house—including cooking dinner two nights a week—starting tonight. It was puzzling how little Becky asked of her kids; they hardly had to work at all besides on their homework and keeping their rooms clean (which they hardly did, anyway). They never, ever even fixed their *own* meals. So naturally it took some doing to convince her to let me cook for the whole lot of them.

But I realized it was my own goose I might have cooked as Becky showed me around the kitchen. It might as well have been the inside of a spaceship.

"Oven, microwave, fridge, *obviously*," she said, pointing out the various "appliances." I'd used the refrigerator, which wasn't all that different from our icebox back home—only electrified—but I'd steered clear of the other two appliances so far. "Chopping knives are in here, normal silverware the next drawer over. Dishwasher, though you won't need that. And just in case, we keep the blender under the counter." She continued on until we'd gone through every nook of the room, showing me a toaster, a mixer, pots, pans, cabinets full of strange spices and mixes and such.

Finally she finished with a flourish. "It's all yours. You sure you're okay?"

"Oh, yes." I nodded furiously.

Once she was gone, I fiddled—turning knobs, pressing buttons, switching switches—mostly for my own curiosity. She hadn't even explained the dishwasher to me, and that was the strangest of all. It was like something purely from imagination. I wished the kids back home could see it—a machine that actually did your chores for you, just like we'd talked about. I was careful to turn everything off as soon as I'd turned it on, and finally I buckled down to work.

I'd decided to make chicken dumplings and gravy, something that had always been simple enough to do. But this night it took forever. Between finding all the right ingredients, and getting the oven to work right, and being extra gentle and careful, it must've taken two or three hours, carrying on way past the usual dinnertime. Nobody complained in the least, though, while they waited. And Becky only poked her head in once to ask if I was finding everything all right.

When I was done, the kitchen was filthy, and I imagined Theo would have bust a gut to see me, covered as I was in broth and flour. But amazingly, the product of all my labors actually looked . . . like chicken and dumplings. Once at the table, everybody smiled and ate it up, commenting on how good it was. It seemed a little underdone to me, but I took their word for it, for they were all smiling up a storm and chewing rapidly.

I had done it. I wished Daddy could have seen it—me acting like a young lady, not just a little girl. After all, I'd cooked for a whole family, hadn't I? And managed not to ruin anything. If things were different, he would have been proud.

I was awoken that night by footsteps pounding down the hall, followed by a slamming of the bathroom door.

"What time is it?" Amelia muttered as I rolled out of bed. Too sleepy and confused to answer, I stumbled through the darkness to the doorway and peered down the moonlit hall. Becky was just opening her bedroom door.

A retching sound came from the bathroom and then a tiny voice. "Mom?"

At that, Becky hurried to the door and threw it open. As she did, a shaft of light fell out onto the hall, showing that Bo had just come out of his room.

We met in front of the bathroom and peered inside. Andrew was leaning over the toilet, retching, and Becky was kneeling behind him, pressing a hand to his forehead.

Bo looked at me and I looked at him, and then he turned and ran downstairs into the kitchen. A moment later there was retching coming from that room, too.

I felt my body go hot and cold. I could only think of one thing—poison. Was my sickness contagious? Had I given it to them somehow? Oh, please, no.

"I don't feel well," came Amelia's voice from behind me. I turned just as she switched on the hall light and blinked at me. "What's going on?"

Finally I turned back toward Becky, hoping she'd be able to answer. I felt a little sick myself, in more than one way.

Becky was standing over the sink now, wetting a small towel and looking a little green. Our eyes met as she turned off the sink. "Food poisoning," she said. "The chicken." Then she turned back to Andrew.

All Becky ever said about the chicken and dumplings incident (besides explaining that everyone would be okay and that it was only undercooked chicken that had caused it all) was, "Maybe cash would be fine."

Her children weren't so mannerly. Bo and Amelia started calling me "Chef Barfo" and asking what was on the menu for the night, then they'd come up with suggestions, like Sick Surprise. At first I didn't get the jokes, and then when I did, I knew they were just teasing, but it still filled me with shame and embarrassment every time—until Amelia seemed to notice and stopped doing it (and got Bo to stop doing it, too).

And then there were the other half-witted things I'd done since I got here and continued to do. For instance, the first time I heard the clothes dryer buzz as I was walking in the downstairs hall, I nearly jumped straight out of my skin. Andrew thought it was the funniest thing he'd ever seen in his life. His brown eyes crinkled up and his face turned red from laughing so darn hard. I was so embarrassed that before I even knew what I was doing, I shook my fist at him.

"Don't make me pop you one, Andrew Aiden." That shut him up quick. Of course, right away I felt awful and apologized my guts out.

The television, of course, was the thing that sucked at my attention the most and kept me feeling backward. I devoured it, though, and anything the shows could tell me about the world. I picked my favorites right away. I didn't like soap operas (too silly), the news (too shocking), or anything violent, which reminded me too much of the Reverend's warnings. I *did* like cartoons—which were positively wonderful—and the funny shows that came on at night, which were mostly about families (and were filled with really handsome people).

More than anything else, it took my mind off of Katie—off of everything, actually—for a few blessed minutes. Every time I sat down to watch it, something new shocked the pants off me.

Watching television with me was what made the Aiden kids laugh the most. Every time something new or strange happened, I would mutter out loud, "Well, I'll be," or just a simple, "No," without even knowing I was doing it. Whenever anything rough happened, even though I knew it was make-believe, I'd pull my shirt right up over my mouth, just an inch from covering my eyes.

Andrew, and even sulky Bo, got in the habit of saying, "Well, I'll be," as a way of teasing. For instance, Andrew would say, "Hey, Bo, did you know birds can fly?" and Bo would get a surprised look on his face and say, "Well, I'll be." And then Andrew would kill himself laughing, and Bo would let out a few dry chuckles under his breath, never even looking at me. I knew they were just being silly, and I soon learned not to get embarrassed by it, but I couldn't bring myself to laugh along with them. I didn't have it in me. I only envied their happiness and wished I could steal a bit of it for me. For Katie and me.

During this time I carefully tucked away every cent I earned, minus the thirty dollars Becky and I settled on, which I gave to her straight out of my pay envelope. It was a lot of money to give up, but my conscience couldn't stand giving her less. I knew enough to realize that I couldn't get room and keep anywhere for near that little. And even though it seemed the Aidens had everything a person could desire, I also knew Becky worried about money, as much as she tried to keep it from me and her children.

Sometimes I could overhear her talking about it on the phone with Mr. Aiden before I'd feel bad for eavesdropping and cover my head with a pillow. I'd be lying in Amelia's room and I would hear her muffled voice through the walls of their bedroom. Usually I could tell it was him 'cause her voice would get soft and she'd start giggling really low, in between all the serious talk.

It was during these talks that I gleaned Becky hadn't told her husband about me. She'd be telling him about something we'd all done together, only she'd leave me out of the story entirely. It made me feel shaky inside because it left me wondering why.

Soon, I told myself, counting up my money in my head and sometimes in my hands, it wouldn't matter, anyway. Soon I'd be gone.

CHAPTER EIGHT

"No, um, you have to shake it like this," Amelia said, gently taking the plastic box in her hand and shaking it to the left, then to the right, and making sure all the letter blocks inside came to rest evenly in their slots.

We were playing Boggle. After getting an explanation of each game the Aidens owned—Trivial Pursuit, Songburst, Boggle, and Monopoly—from Amelia, I'd opted for this one as the only game that I'd have half a chance of not looking stupid at. I'd always been a good speller.

It was March 6, the kind of night not fit for man or beast. But inside the Aiden house the snow and ice were only a picture through the window. Inside, it couldn't have been warmer or more pleasant. Country-style music was blaring from the radio in the kitchen, and Bo had built a fire in the fireplace.

Amelia cast a timid eye on me while she shook. It wasn't like her to be timid, but for the past few days that's exactly what she'd been—not so chattery, not grabbing me by the hand or the arm all the time and gushing about this or that. I guess there were only so many times you could pull away, or turn your back, or give a one-word answer before even someone as friendly as Amelia got the message. She was still friendly, but she seemed less *sure* of my friendship. She maybe even seemed a little hurt. I was relieved she was backing off of me a little, but it also made me feel a little . . . *bad.*

"I hope he's not out there traveling," Becky said from her chair. We knew, of course, she meant Mr. Aiden. He was supposed to be home in two days—a fact that made me more than a little nervous. What would he think of me living here, with his family? What kinds of questions would he ask?

"I'm always fine the first week or so," she added. "It's the second that makes me antsy. I hate these long trips."

But tonight it was clear she was making an effort to be extra happy. It was Becky's birthday, and just like back home, everybody gave her gifts—a CD called *Celtic Escape* from Amelia and a pair of velvet gloves from Andrew and Bo. Even I had managed to give her a flower-printed scarf I had found at the Hand-Me-Down store. Of course, in Dogwood the gifts had always been homemade. But the spirit was the same.

And then Becky, being Becky, had turned it into a celebration for all of us. She'd cooked a special dinner—steak—and afterward handed out mugs of apple cider, forbidding us to head for the TV. She'd declared it a family night and said we'd just have to spend time talking and laughing with one another like civilized human beings. I thought that was funny, considering I'd never met a family more civilized than the Aidens.

As we went on with our game, Becky gave us a mysterious grin, then disappeared down the hallway. When she came back, she had a big paper bag in her arms.

"For you," she said over and over as she pulled out these shiny boxes and handed one to each of us. She got to me last.

I watched the other kids to see what they did, and when I saw them tearing the shiny covering off their packages, I did the same. In another motion I had it open. It was a box filled with candy, of all different sizes and colors.

Becky seemed to be watching me closely, and when she saw my face, her own lit up. "They were left over from Valentine's Day. I got them on sale," she said, looking sheepish.

"Thank you!" I breathed, thrilled. Not so much because I love sweets (which I do), but because it was such a nice thought to give it to me. I didn't have the slightest idea what "on sale" meant. Bo and Andrew hadn't said anything, but they were already in the process of trading pieces. I immediately made a mental promise never to eat these as long as I lived, they were so pretty. But then no sooner had I promised than the urge came over me and I popped one in my mouth. It was heavenly.

At some point, as we were all digging into our sweets greedily (except for Amelia, who didn't seem to care about candy either way and offered me hers), the song on the radio changed.

The rhythm plugged along like a lopsided pony in a nice,

happy way, with all sorts of instruments playing at once. Then a man with a twangy voice joined in. *"All my exes live in Texas. Texas is a place I'd really looove to be. . . ."*

In a flash Becky grabbed Bo from his seat and began to swing him around the room. "I *love* this song," she said as Bo rolled his eyes. She lifted his arm, making an arc that she then spun herself under.

Amelia was laughing and pointing at Bo, who was smiling a little despite himself. Andrew had already jumped up and was trying to grab Becky's hand, which Bo gladly handed over. This time it was Andrew who swung under Becky's arm—back, forth, back, forth, till it seemed that he must collapse from dizziness. His mouth formed an *o,* like he was trying to look serious but suppressing a grin at the same time.

"That's why I hang my hat in Tennessee. . . ."

Finally he stumbled away, and then Becky was reaching out her hand to me. She folded her fingers in, out, in, out, motioning me toward her.

"Ohhh," I said, leaning back farther in my seat and crossing my arms over my box of chocolates. "Ohhh, nooo."

But Becky had already grabbed my hand and, with some help from Amelia pushing from behind, was pulling me up, up, up.

"I remember that ole Frio River where I learned to swim . . ." the man on the radio sang, Becky singing along with him.

Somehow she managed to snap me out, straightening my

arm, and in another moment she had me spinning in toward her. Then I felt myself tipping backward, and I could hear everybody laughing as I was yanked back up.

This isn't half bad, I was thinking. I began to forget I had no earthly idea how to dance right, and I started laughing along with everyone else. I even started to try keeping rhythm to the music like Becky, and it actually wasn't so hard.

None of us heard the front door open. Even without the radio blaring I doubt we would have, seeing as we were laughing so hard. Nobody noticed anything until the music stopped, and we all turned to see a heavy, bearded man standing in the doorway of the kitchen. In his right hand was a giant spray of flowers. *Stargazer lilies,* I noted absently.

Becky, with a huge smile that lit up her whole face, let go of my hand and ran over to throw her arms around his neck. Andrew, too, jumped at him in a flash. Bo followed, a bit more reserved but smiling. Amelia hobbled over and—after casting a tentative, warm glance back at me, as if to include me—gave him a tight hug and a loud kiss on the cheek.

"Hey, Dad," she said.

"We didn't expect you till Monday," Becky said, pulling back from her hug and folding one hand over the other in her way. She looked relieved, exuberant, and nervous at the same time.

"Seemed wrong to miss your birthday if I could at all help it." Mr. Aiden handed her the bouquet of flowers and kissed her on the lips. Then he fixed a casual smile on me over his wife's shoulder. "Who's this?" he asked.

"Oh." Becky looked over her shoulder. She grabbed my sleeve and pulled me forward, then put an arm around my shoulders. She was smiling, but it looked forced. "This is Glory—she's staying with us."

"Nice to meet you, Glory," he said, putting out his giant hand. I shook it but didn't say a word. He was the burliest man I'd ever seen. Not so tall as my own daddy, but bigger around the arms, the middle. I wondered how he could get so big just by driving a truck around. "You're spending the night with Amelia?"

I looked at Becky for an answer.

"Well, honey, I've been meaning to talk to you about it," Becky said, after holding my nervous gaze for a moment. "I was gonna tell you over the phone before you got back." Becky took his hand. "Can we discuss it later? I wanna find out about your trip. . . ."

Mr. Aiden gave Becky a confused frown, obviously surprised that there was a whole story behind my presence here. He paused for a moment, then finally responded to Becky's pleading gaze by enveloping her in a hug. "Sure. Nice to meet you, Glory," he called over her head. I tried not to let my nervousness show as I replied with a meek, "You, too, sir."

Lying awake in the trundle bed later that night, I listened to Becky and Mr. Aiden—the hum of their voices looping and rising and dipping—in the bedroom next to me. For several minutes I lay there, letting the sound, which reminded me of *my* mama and daddy, lull me. But before I could drift off, something changed. The voices suddenly took on a deep, serious tone. My body tensed up. They were arguing. I trained my ears toward the wall.

I knew I shouldn't listen, but a voice inside told me to be alert. Now and then the word *she* would come up and I knew in my gut they were arguing about me.

The next few days only helped to back up my suspicions. Becky seemed happier, mostly, than she had been before— humming to herself, moving about the store with an extra bounce in her step. But when it came to me, she was awkward.

Mr. Aiden was always there now when we got home in the evenings, and life at the house changed because of it. The kids were less rambunctious—not perfectly behaved, still, but calmer and more orderly. Even Becky did things in a less slapdash way. If she and the kids were the core of the Aiden home, Mr. Aiden seemed to be the structure that held up the walls.

Still, it would have all been quite pleasant—even with my shyness around a new person—if there wasn't also that added *something*. I felt it when I sat down at dinner or when I happened to pass Mr. Aiden in the hallway. There was tension in the air. And it somehow centered on me.

"You said your mother has what kind of illness again?" Mr. Aiden would ask. Or, "What part of Boston does your grandmother live in?" or, "What kind of work are you doing for school?" And instead of being polite and just accepting my answers for what they were, he'd ask another question and another. I'd been lucky with the others, I figured. Anybody could have asked the questions Mr. Aiden was asking me now. But nobody had, and now I realized I was poorly prepared.

And the worst of it was, he made no secret of the fact that he didn't believe me. He didn't say it. He just stared at me hard and kept saying, "Hmmm," to all of my answers.

"Nicholas, quit pestering her," Becky would say, leaning over the back of his chair and putting her hands on his shoulders. But it wasn't that simple.

It made me think of one of my mama's favorite expressions: "What a tangled web we weave, when first we practice to deceive." It was just like that—like we were all three tangled up in a web. Becky and I were the bugs. She wasn't telling me the whole truth about how much of my story she actually believed, and I wasn't telling anyone much of anything. And Mr. Aiden was the spider, catching us in our lies.

We were having something called chicken stir-fry. Andrew, a fussy eater, had sifted through the vegetables and rice and decided it wasn't worth eating. He only nibbled at the chicken bits, which seemed to annoy Becky to no end. I'd never seen her in such a foul mood. It made what I was about to say even harder.

It took me all the way until dinner was almost over. But I didn't want to wait any longer. If Mr. Aiden was nervous about me, I wanted to put his mind at ease before he did something about it.

"I wanted to tell you . . ." I said, stabbing at a spear of broccoli on my plate and lifting it to my mouth in a desperate try to look less nervous than I felt. "I've almost got enough money saved. I wanted to say that come next Friday, since Thursday's payday and all, I'll be leaving."

Becky dropped her fork with a clatter. Amelia put both hands on the table at the sides of her plate. Only Mr. Aiden looked unmoved. I plunged ahead.

"I appreciate your kindness so much. Only, I'll have enough money then, and I really need to get going."

I popped some broccoli in my mouth. Why did I feel so bad right now? Shouldn't I be happy? Not wanting to look up, I stabbed at another vegetable and another and shoved them into my mouth.

"No," Becky said suddenly. She looked at her husband, and he looked back at her. "I'm sorry, but no. I can't let you do that."

Becky was clutching her napkin, and Mr. Aiden was looking at her, shaking his head like she had better not do whatever it was she was about to do. I looked from one of them to the other now, unable to look away. They were telling each other something with their eyes, I could see. My mama and daddy used to do the same thing sometimes.

"We talked about this, Becky," he said. "Don't do this."

"No, Nick. I'm sorry, but this just isn't right."

What were they talking about?

"Glory," Becky said, her shoulders sagging as she let out a deep breath. "We want you to stay with us. We want you to live with us. For good."

Live with us. For good.

Whatever crunched-up vegetables I had in my mouth had just gone down the wrong pipe and I was choking. Bo leaned over and patted my back, hard. I took a deep swallow.

"What?" I asked, my throat getting tight and scratchy. But it wasn't the sickness. It was just pure shock.

Mr. Aiden suddenly stood up and threw his napkin down on his plate. Then he stomped away. Becky watched him go. When he was gone, she turned her attention back to me. "Kids? Can you leave Glory and me alone, please?"

Amelia, Bo, and Andrew straggled out of the room, looking sheepish, like they already knew, too. Amelia patted me on the shoulder as she went. Then it was just me and Becky. She scooted into the spot next to me and took my hand.

"Look, honey, I don't know your story, but I do know it's not what you say it is." She paused, searching my eyes with her own for confirmation. Apparently she got it 'cause she went on. "I know you don't go *home* when you say you do. I know you don't get 'home schooled.' And I'm not mad at you for lying. You're probably doing what you have to. But Glory, do you really have anyone to go to in Boston?"

I started to nod, but in the face of Becky's honest stare, it turned into a head shake.

"I figured not. And your family?"

I shook my head again, this time more passionately.

"Okay, okay," she said. "I trust you. I figure you have your reasons. But listen." This time she took my chin in her hands. "You're not alone. You have me. And the kids. And Nick will come around. We care about you, Glory. We don't want you to go. And seeing as you *have* nowhere to go, I think you should stay. We can look after you. Get you enrolled in school. We can figure out a way to make it work."

Now I was speechless. I couldn't even shake my head anymore. "I . . ."

Becky nodded, waiting on my next words.

"I . . . I need to go for a walk," I blurted, standing up and releasing myself from Becky's grip.

In another second I was out on the street without my coat, trying to stomp the messy feelings inside out through my feet. They knew. They all knew. And they wanted me to stay.

The whole conversation sliced through my heart as I went through it time and time again. Really, I should have been relieved. The Aidens knew that I'd been lying, and they hadn't told anyone. They hadn't called the authorities. In fact, they'd invited me to stay, which was nice, even though it was impossible.

So why didn't I feel relieved?

Despite the cold, I stayed out till way past dark. I knew that it was rude and that Becky would be worried. But I just couldn't go back. I was too nervous to have her asking me more questions I wasn't ready to answer. And I was too worried about seeing Mr. Aiden, who—judging from his behavior at the table—probably hated me.

I strayed back and forth past the house a few times, and finally, when I saw the Aidens' bedroom light go out, I entered through the front door as quietly as possible.

To my surprise, Mr. Aiden was sitting in the living room, waiting for me, a single lamp casting a ring of light around his chair and his big form.

"Good night," I mumbled, starting toward the stairs. But his voice stopped me.

"Glory, please come have a seat." I turned back toward him. I couldn't tell from the expression on his face whether he was angry or just tired. Reluctantly I walked back into the living room and sat on the edge of the couch, as far across the room as possible, my hands folded.

"It's a little late to be getting back from a walk, don't you think?"

I nodded. We stared at each other.

"Glory, don't get the wrong idea. I think you're a sweet girl, and my family, obviously, thinks you're the best thing since sliced bread."

I just sat.

"Becky and I know you haven't been telling the truth—Becky, of course, longer than me. And from the look of you, we both can see you've been through a lot."

He paused and waited for a reply, but I said nothing.

"Fortunately or unfortunately, my wife is a bit less practical than I am. She wants to just forget your past, whatever it is, and let you start a new life here with us. But I can't do that.

"Glory, I'd like you to stay. It's what my family wants. But it's more complicated than that. So you're just going to have to bear with us for a while. In the meantime," he said, clearing his throat and sitting up straighter. "Becky and I have discussed it, and we'd like to have a dinner next Thursday. A belated welcome to the town, or I guess a going-away party if it ends up that way. We'd invite some of our friends so they could meet you; we can even tell them you're a relative if it would make you feel more comfortable."

I swallowed. Was I imagining it, or was he avoiding my eyes now? Something about this moment seemed even more nerve-racking than it had to be. Mr. Aiden obviously wanted me to say something—anything—but I felt stuck, and my gut told me something was off. Maybe it was just the thought of meeting a group of strangers all at once, who'd be coming here just to meet *me*. Maybe it was the thought that the Aidens had just assumed I'd *want* to stay with them when I shouldn't, I couldn't.

But how could I refuse Mr. Aiden's offer of a party? Especially after all the Aidens had done for me?

"Thank you, sir," I said, to my hands instead of to him. "That would be nice."

We headed upstairs and said our good nights to each other, and after he'd disappeared into his room, I tiptoed back downstairs—too riled up to get in bed. I flicked on the television set in the basement, turned down the volume knob so the sound was low, and, using the buttons on top, moved through the channels until I'd settled on a movie. A very handsome man was sitting by a bed where a woman lay, her face pale, long ginger hair splayed behind her on the white pillow. She had tears in her eyes, and there was the saddest music you could imagine playing as they held hands. Clearly she was sick—even dying, it looked like. A coincidence, I guess. I let my mind sink into the movie.

I felt bad for the man who loved her. She'd be drifting away, into sleep or heaven or wherever she was headed. (I wasn't sure anymore where that might be.) But it was the person beside her who'd be left behind.

I wondered if she wished they'd never met. Just so that he wouldn't miss her when she was gone.

CHAPTER
NINE

"Glory, I've heard a lot about you."

Mr. Levi Bushfield smiled and shook my hand.

"Nice to meet you," I replied, but I didn't mean it. Becky was in the kitchen cooking, so my eyes searched the room for Amelia. Funny how, amongst all these strangers, I suddenly longed for her company.

About twelve guests had arrived for the party—Mr. and Mrs. Aiden's friends and their kids, all carrying bowls and platters and baskets of food, all here to meet me. The table was laid with a festive red tablecloth and covered with goodies—what the guests had brought and also what Becky had cooked. All the lights were on, and the fire roared in the fireplace.

I'd agreed to stay another week. Not because I was thinking of staying for good, but because Becky had begged me to, and I didn't feel I could refuse her. But the fear of getting sick between now and then continued to nag at me. My head was swimming, my cheeks felt warm, and when I touched my skin, it was moist. But whether it was the heat from the fire or something much deeper and more worrisome, I didn't know. One thing I did know, though, was that I was very, very nervous.

"Becky didn't tell me you were such a pretty young lady," Mr. Bushfield added. I hardly heard. For the last few minutes I hadn't seen Amelia anywhere. I would have settled for Andrew, even Bo—any familiar face—but they seemed to have disappeared.

"Thank you," I said to Mr. Bushfield absently, finally turning my gaze back to rest on him. Thick-rimmed spectacles. A short haircut with the fringe combed to one side. He was the neatest, tidiest man I'd ever seen, with a pointed, intelligent stare that was focused squarely on me. I squirmed, shifting from one foot to the other. Something about him made me feel uncomfortable. Even more than I was already feeling.

"Excuse me," I said. Before he could protest, I moved across the room and ducked into the bathroom. His comment about me being pretty had given me the idea to go check myself in the mirror, as an excuse to get in a room by myself for a few minutes. Once inside, I locked the door behind me and turned on the light. Then I rested my hands on the counter, on either side of the sink, and gazed at my reflection.

I was wearing the blue dress I had bought. Amelia said it set off my dark eyes and looked nice with the hint of lipstick she had applied. (*I'm sorry, Daddy,* I had said silently, a pinch of heartache taking over for a few moments.) It certainly was fetching, I had to admit. I understood now, a little better, why some women actually *liked* wearing dresses. There was a strange, magical feeling that came with being in one that fit so nicely. Amelia had wrapped my hair in a cunning bun that sat low on the back of my head, securing it with these little clips called barrettes. She'd left a few wisps here and there, which she'd said were a great "frame for my face." But pretty? That would be going too far.

I was still very pale. And the skin under my eyes was a bit bluish. I didn't look well—not healthy and happy like Amelia. And my eyes had this timid jackrabbit wideness to them. But I looked better than usual. "Okay," I said to the mirror. I took a couple of deep breaths, palms still flat on the counter. Then I headed back out into the crowd.

I passed by the kitchen. Becky was leaning over a bowl of cake batter. When she saw me, she motioned me forward with a tilt of her head.

"Have a taste." She ran my finger along the batter-covered prong of her mixing gadget, then left me to lick it off.

"S'good," I said. "What's in it?"

Becky looked at me in that way she had, up from under her eyebrows. "The usual. Sugar, flour, chocolate. Once I get this in the oven, I'm free to socialize."

I nodded.

"But you look like you wish you were free to hide in the kitchen."

I tried to smile bravely. A look, somehow a guilty look, drew her mouth down for a moment. Then she patted my side.

"I was shy when I was younger." I snorted to show I didn't believe her. "No, no, I was. But you'll soon find there's no reason to be. And these folks, Glory, they only wish good things for you. They're our friends." Her look was meaningful, like she was saying more than she was saying, and it was also a little sheepish. Again, like the other night with Mr. Aiden, I had the feeling in my gut that something here was not what it seemed.

I leaned my back against the counter, both hands resting on either side of me and my elbows tucked up behind my back. "I know, Becky. I really appreciate it. Your having this for me and all."

Again Becky's mouth nipped down at the edges.

"Our pleasure, honey. I hope . . . I hope it can mark a new beginning for us. I hope we can work it out so you'll stay."

I felt myself blushing and stared down at my shoes, bought new for the occasion. I didn't know what to say to that. Why didn't I just say I couldn't? Why didn't I just tell her, "No, thank you," and not let her go on wondering? For the life of me, I didn't know.

"Now, go on," Becky said, patting me again. "Your public awaits."

When we finally sat down to dinner, there were eighteen people in all. The Aidens and me, plus their friends the Walshes, the Sissons, the Gabriels, and Levi Bushfield and his wife. There were two or three kids close to my age and a few that were younger, but I wasn't seated near them. Mr. Aiden had moved the kitchen table out into the common room and then brought in another table from outside—so we were all divided. Most of the kids were seated together at one, while I was with the grown-ups at another—right between Becky and Mr. Bushfield.

Before us lay a feast. Folks began digging in right away, which, as usual, made me feel a little odd for not saying grace. But then, I'd also given up grace by that point. I'd given up praying entirely.

Bowls and dishes started circling the table this way and that, overlapping one another and sometimes clinking together. Feeling slightly queasy, I only took tiny smidgens of each, and that only to be polite. I'd have to force it all down since I was too nervous for my taste buds to work properly, anyway. Especially because of Levi Bushfield, who was asking me too many questions.

"Do they have feasts like this back home, Glory?" he asked, sipping at a glass filled with clear, yellowish liquid. I looked at my own glass. No yellow liquid—just water.

"No, sir," I said. "I mean, well, sometimes." I took a sip of water.

"And where is it that you're from?"

I cleared my throat. "Ummm, Clifton. I'm from a town called Clifton. You probably haven't heard of it. It's small," I added.

Mr. Bushfield squinted at me and thought for a moment. "No, can't say that I have. What's it like?"

What's it like? My imagination hadn't stretched that far yet. Nobody I'd used the lie on so far had asked me what Clifton was *like,* at least so bluntly.

"What's it like?" I stalled. "Well, you know, it's just a normal town. Like usual."

"No, tell me. What's usual?"

I made an attempt at a laugh. "Oh, you know, cars. Houses. Um, very small."

"Yeah, you said that. Tell me, how does your family like living there?"

"Oh, I guess okay. I mean, my whole family likes it fine."

"Does that mean you have brothers and sisters?"

"Oh, no."

"Becky said you didn't. But then when you said your whole family—"

"I meant my mama and me," I interrupted. My stomach gave out a low whine.

"Right. Of course. Well, I'm very sorry your mother is ill." Was I imagining how uncomfortable this all was? If Mr. Bushfield was suspicious of me, I couldn't think what reasons he had to start with or why in the world he would care. "Becky told me."

"Thank you," I said then, wondering what Becky had told all these people about me. I looked at her helplessly, but she was busy chattering with one of her friends. Then I stared down at my plate and willed the tears to creep back behind my eyes. I couldn't help it—I just felt like crying.

When I looked up again, I was relieved to find Mr. Bushfield turned away and talking to his wife. Amelia and I locked eyes across the room, and she grinned sympathetically. I smiled back, grateful, appreciating her very much all of a sudden—and feeling badly for how I'd treated her. I had to get hold of myself. Everything was going to be all right.

By dessert time Mr. Bushfield had asked me several more questions about myself. I decided he was the most nosy, on top of the most tidy, person I'd ever met. But I managed to get through his questions somehow. I was especially careful not to contradict anything I'd said before, and I tried to be as vague as possible about everything else. Maybe I was an even better liar than I thought because after a while, he seemed satisfied and stopped prodding me so much.

The rest of the guests and I—at least the grown-ups sitting around me—got along fine. Better than fine. Folks commented on my good manners (which was funny since I was considered the orneriest, most unmannerly girl in Dogwood). They said that I was pretty and that I had a lovely southern accent, and I was just overflowing with the compliments—which wasn't something I was used to. Especially having had Katie as a best friend; all people's compliments had always gone to her. I would have rathered it still be that way. But it was nice all the same.

Until Becky started clearing the table. "Anne, you wanna hand me your wineglass?" she asked. She was leaning over my shoulder, picking up plates and glasses on either side of me.

It took all the will I could muster to keep sitting there, looking calm, while I took in what Becky had said. Wine. That stuff in Levi's glass was wine. They were all drinking spirits! And not like at church. They were drinking whole glasses full. And out in the open for everyone to see. I wanted to shout—didn't they know it was a sin? That it made you do stupid, horrible things?

I tried to pretend it wasn't happening. I pushed the memory of that night at the lake with Katie out of my mind for fear it would make me fall apart right there in front of everyone.

"You want cake?" I turned around to see Andrew, helping his mom by bringing out dessert.

"Yes, please," I said, reaching for the plate without really wanting to and giving Andrew a fake smile. "Thank you."

Dessert was followed by coffee and tea, and by that time it seemed like we'd been at the table for three days. I'd relaxed by then. I'd pushed the wine out of my mind as just one more thing about the modern world I didn't understand, right beside cooking equipment and the workings of television. Any meaning beyond that, I decided to ignore. These were kind people. Good people. And so far, they hadn't done one stupid thing.

But now I was getting bored. My toes itched. I curled my fingers in and out, waiting for the whole thing to be over.

Finally Becky retreated into the kitchen to do the washing up, and the other women followed suit. The men got up and gravitated toward the couches on the opposite side of the room. *Well,*

I thought, irked, *I guess some things don't change no matter where you go.* But helping out was the least I could do, even though it was unfair that the boys didn't have to, so I followed the ladies into the kitchen, only to be shooed out by Becky, saying I was still a guest. She sent Amelia hobbling after me to keep me company. Again, amongst all these strangers, I was glad. For once I wanted for Amelia to stick as close to me as possible.

Taking the lead, she propped herself on the edge of her daddy's seat, pulling me down beside her. Sitting there, I could understand how people felt uncomfortable around my daddy, when I myself had never been able to understand it. Amelia seemed perfectly at ease with hers, but to me he was as frightening as a great grizzly bear. I was stiff as I leaned back and listened to the men talk of all sorts of boring men's matters.

Amelia waited for a lull in the conversation, then put her hand on her father's shoulder.

"Why don't you play, Dad?"

Mr. Aiden looked confused for a second, then shook his head. "Nah . . ."

"Nah, what?" Becky was standing beside us now, drying her hands on a dish towel. "C'mon, honey."

To my confusion, everybody started goading Mr. Aiden on, and Amelia said, "Pleeease," in her sweetest voice. Please do what, I didn't know.

Finally Mr. Aiden threw up his hands in defeat. "Will you go get it?" he asked. Amelia was gone and back in a moment or two, holding in her left hand . . . a harmonica.

Mr. Aiden? Was he going to play it? I could only smile at how unfitting the idea seemed.

Still, he put it to his lips, cupped his hands around the front of the instrument, and started playing. And to my amazement, he was excellent. Some people clapped as he blew his way through a lively riff, and all the chatter in the room turned to calls of encouragement as the women trailed out of the kitchen. When he was finished, the whole room burst into applause, and then he sailed into another, more soulful tune, his eyes closing tight and his forehead scrunching up.

I'd never imagined such sweet, delicate sounds could come out of a big man like Mr. Aiden, and I started clapping and keeping time with the rhythm as people called out requests. "Play 'Fox on the Run.'" "'Honeycomb.'" People shouted and hooted.

Gosh. How many nights had we spent in Dogwood like this, listening to someone or other—usually my uncle Cecil—play the harmonica? In the long late winter months—January, February, March—when it was too nasty out and all we could do was gather by the fire. And although those had mostly been holy songs and the ones Mr. Aiden was playing seemed more unpredictable and lively, the reaction was the same. Everybody was merry as could be.

"Glory?"

Suddenly I was roused from my thoughts to realize that the music had stopped, and Mr. Aiden was looking at me expectantly. "What?" I asked Amelia, for it was she who had spoken.

Amelia repeated her question. "I was saying that since it's your night, you should make a request."

"Um." I looked around the room. Some folks were waiting for me to answer, and some were just chattering and laughing. Levi Bushfield and I locked eyes for a moment. "Um." I turned to Mr. Aiden. He was looking at me happily, friendly.

"Do you know 'Down by the Meadow'?" I asked, doubting he'd know it. But without even a pause Mr. Aiden put his lips to his harmonica.

Even on the first few notes the back of my neck tingled. A vision of home hit me with such force that it seemed like the music had flicked some electric switch inside my heart. It brought to my mind a night that even a few minutes ago, I couldn't have remembered properly if I'd tried. I saw my uncle, an old man by then, crouched over his harmonica, my sister Teresa resting on her knees beside his chair, little me and slightly less little Theo on the rug cross-legged, and Mama and Daddy, I think, standing by grinning—though I couldn't remember exactly where.

It was something familiar—like I said, we spent many nights sitting around listening to the harmonica. But for some reason, on that night I could remember looking around the room and thinking: *This is special. Tomorrow this night will be gone.* It was perfect, that's what it was. It was a time when I felt perfectly content, when I wasn't yearning for something more or for things to be different. That night, despite everything, I felt like I was in the very place God intended me to be.

This isn't perfect, I thought, looking around the room full of strangers, catching Mr. Bushfield staring at me (he quickly looked away) and watching Mr. Aiden blowing his own notes in his own different way, nothing like Uncle Cecil, and still remembering all that I had lost and all that I would lose soon. *But it's nice.*

I leaned into the chair and forgot about being uncomfortable. I forgot about yesterday, and tomorrow, and the limited number of tomorrows after that. And I just let myself drift in the moment, floating on the notes and feeling, almost, happy.

Long after everyone was in their rooms—asleep, or so I thought—I sat by the fire and watched the last of the embers in the fireplace glow and burn away.

The night had been a success. Somehow, for some miraculous reason, everyone liked me. Becky had said so, and even if she hadn't, I could tell by the way people had hugged me and welcomed me and said they were glad to have me. Mr. Aiden had looked on me with smiling eyes the whole night, in addition to playing my song. Even Bo—sulky, quiet Bo—had sent a grin my way once or twice. It was more than I could understand or bear.

I would have almost said the Aidens . . . loved me. Crazy as that may sound, on account of my not being with them very long and on account of me being such a bad person in general and having done so much wrong.

They don't know you, Glory, I told myself. *They don't know what kind of wrong it is you've done.*

But it made me feel good, anyway.

I kept staring into the fire, unable to think of going to bed. The Aidens, at the very least, cared. Somehow I'd come here a stranger and now I had these people who wanted to take care of me.

It was almost a shame I had to go away.

I did *have to* go away, didn't I?

What if I stayed? What if I spent my last days here with people who liked me and wanted to look after me? It would be selfish, sure, to let them love me when they'd soon lose me. And I'd have to keep my secrets that whole time. But they had one another to lean on. I had no one. Shouldn't I have someone to lean on, too?

Over the last week I had finally earned enough to get my ticket to Boston, plus a bit extra. But I hadn't really allowed myself to think about it, and now I realized why. I, at least part of me, wanted to take Becky up on this new offer. Part of me wanted it really, terribly bad.

Oh, Katie, I said silently. *This would be so much easier if I knew you were watching me and seeing what I do. It would be so much easier to leave here. Do you even care if I make it to Boston? Would you even know?*

Before, it had been unimaginable to ask this question

because believing in the answer as yes was what was keeping me going. But now, I wondered. Did she?

I didn't expect a reply from Katie like I'd expected one from God. No matter what Katie's spirit did, she was beyond reproach. And apparently she chose to do nothing.

Sighing, I kneaded at the fabric of my dress that draped across my lap. Was I actually considering this? To stay here and have a life—a short one, but a short, *happy* one? Or maybe not happy, but happi*er*. Happier than being alone in some strange, giant city miles and miles away. Happier than having no money and no place to stay and, most important, no one who cared. If I stayed here, I could just pretend. That I would live longer than a few months and that Dogwood had never happened and that the Aidens had always been my family and that nothing I'd ever done was so very wrong. I could forget about God and how I'd been hurt by Him. Like the Aidens, I wouldn't even think too much about God.

But even if I didn't pretend, a life here would be better than anything I could hope to find in Boston. Luck had brought me Becky and the others, and it wasn't likely to strike again.

Maybe, I thought, standing up and smoothing out my skirt. *Maybe I will stay.*

I was surprised to see, on my way to the bathroom to brush my teeth, that the light from Becky's bedroom was shining under her door. When I came out again, it was still on, and I could hear that she and Mr. Aiden were talking. I should have kept going. I should have crawled into bed and respected their privacy. But my feet rooted me to the spot, and my stomach flipped, and my skin got tingly and prickly. Somehow I knew they were talking about me.

I leaned in to listen.

"Rebecca, can you think practically for just one second?" Mr. Aiden's voice.

"Oh, all you ever are is practical. She's just a little girl, Nick."

I felt sick. "Look, I've tried to be understanding. But you heard what Levi said. She's most likely a runaway. She has a *family* somewhere, Beck. We can't just up and adopt her. We couldn't even if we wanted to."

"Well, if she does have a family, she obviously had a reason to leave," Becky snapped. "Have you looked at her? I mean, really looked at her? She looks . . ." Becky trailed off, and I wondered what she meant to say. "If she has a family who cares about her, where are they?"

Silence.

"Huh?" she prodded.

"That's what Lee's gonna find out. Lots of kids have their fingerprints on record, and there are other ways. He'll find out, and then we'll see. If her family is no good, Child Welfare won't send her back there."

"Child Welfare." At those two words I shivered.

Becky snorted. "Yeah, but they won't place her here, either. It takes *years*, Nick, for stuff like this to work out. Glory might be eighteen before we could get it all straightened out and then . . ."

My legs had become unglued. At some point they had started moving, and Becky's voice drifted into a mumble as I crept into Amelia's bedroom and crawled under the covers, still in my dress. For what seemed like hours, and probably was, I lay there frozen until I was absolutely sure there wasn't a sound in the house and everyone had gone to sleep. Then I crawled back out of bed and reached under the mattress. My hand knew exactly where the money was and how much of it I had. $197.38. Enough for the ticket to Boston and a bit more. I hadn't given Becky the money for this week, and after debating for a moment, I reluctantly laid it on my pillow.

The moonlight shone through Amelia's fluffy curtains as I leaned over her desk, found a paper and pen, and scribbled a quick note:

Dear Aiden Family,
    Thank you for being so kind to me, even when I lied to you. I will never forget you. And I'm sorry.

                                                            Glory

CHAPTER
TEN

The bus glided through the darkness, in and out of clusters of light that must have been towns, smooth as a rocket. Tucked way back in the last seat of the bus to Boston, leaning against a big glass window, I could feel the wheels churning under my feet and, despite all that was going through my head, it comforted me.

It smoothed out the excitement of being on a bus and on my way to Boston and the sadness of leaving the Aidens. And thankfully, it smoothed out the guilt of, this very night, having considered giving up on my promise to get to Boston and pretending my life before—Katie included—had never existed. The wheels groaned evenly beneath me, the floor heated the soles of my feet, and the motion rocked me . . . and it all seemed less unsettling. Or like it belonged to another world, much different than the safe, dark, quiet one I was in now. We were rushing away from it all—away from being caught, away from Levi Bushfield, away from everything and toward something that, for now, could still seem like a dream in the distance.

The bus was almost empty. Besides me there were five

people on it altogether, and nobody had so much as blinked an eye at a thirteen-year-old girl with a knapsack and pale blue circles under her eyes. I watched through the window as the shadows of towns loomed out at me, then fields lit by the moon, then scattered buildings with lights flickering. I couldn't tell whether they belonged to towns that were bigger than Shadow Tree or smaller. It seemed to go on for hours, and somewhere, I fell asleep.

I was awakened, who knows how much later, by the whistling whir of the doors opening. Three people trickled toward the front to leave.

"Is this Boston?" I asked a man with the darkest skin I'd ever seen and short, snow white hair.

He shook his head. "New York," he said, and continued off the bus.

I looked out the window, hoping to see New York—but we were in a building of some sort. New York was another big city, I knew—even bigger than Boston—but all I could see were lots of buses and gray, blank walls.

"Oh." I put my hand to my forehead. My brain was spinning somewhere behind it. I suddenly felt so ill. Not a coughing kind of ill, but the swimmy feeling I'd had at the Aidens' party. Even in the woods, I hadn't felt this *exhausted*. I felt hollow inside and like I'd be content to sit on this bus forever if only that meant I'd never have to move another muscle.

I leaned my head back against the window as another string of passengers began to trickle on, but luckily none of them sat by me. Struggling to stay awake, I forced my eyes wide open, but it was like my head was filled with lead. And before I knew it, everything was blackness again, and I was asleep.

When I woke again, it was light, and we were surrounded by fields alternated with giant walls of rock so smooth and straight, they looked like they'd been sliced to fit the road. There was no snow at all.

I rubbed at my face and moved my tongue, which felt dry and pasty, around my mouth. My stomach set up a loud protest, and I wished, not for the first time, that I'd been smart enough to bring some food.

Oh, God, I longed for home. For the hills and the well-worn paths and the houses and, of course, the familiar faces. Would I ever stop longing for all of it?

But this, this would make things better. Boston would make it all seem worth it. I was going to get there, for real. I pulled the list I had made of things to do in Boston out of the front pocket of my knapsack, where I'd tucked it weeks ago.

The things I have to do in Boston:
Ride the swan boats
Eat in a restaurant with a real waiter
Read a newspaper all the way through

Go to the top floor of a skyscraper
Ride in a taxi
Be happy

Was there anything I wanted to add?

A vision came back to me of the church Mrs. Johansen had shown me a picture of—the one with her and her grandmother standing in front. I thought about the nearby bakery she had talked about, saying how she was always so happy to go to church because it meant going to that bakery afterward. Would I even be able to find these places?

I pulled out a pencil I had also tucked away. *Go to Mrs. Johansen's church,* I wrote. It was a big thing, to put something on my list. I couldn't take it lightly. It meant a promise—to Katie—that I would do something for her. It meant being a part of the whole of my Boston dream and what that dream signified.

As we hurtled on forward, the empty fields slowly turned into scattered plots of land, and these turned into roads and house-lined streets. And these turned into busier and busier streets lined with houses that got to be so close together, they practically bumped into each other.

"Excuse me, ma'am?" I said, leaning toward a passenger two seats across from me. "Are we coming up on Boston?" When she nodded, my heart leapt into my mouth.

I smushed my face right up against the window now,

anticipation and nausea curled up inside me as a tight ball, ready to unravel with the first sight of the city. A dark smudge appeared in the distance ahead, followed by another and another. I desperately tried to look as far forward as possible. The sick, tired feeling of earlier was completely gone.

The dark smudges were impossibly high in the air, and they soon took on shapes. Roof and window shapes, gleaming glass reflecting the sun. My Lord, they were buildings!

A rustling started through the crowd on the bus—zippers and clicks and such. A few folks shifted restlessly in their seats. I kept my cheek against the window as Boston towered up before me.

I will never again see something this beautiful, I said to myself. *I will never have this moment again.*

I savored it for all it was worth.

"Miss, this is South Station."

The bus driver himself was standing above me now. Somehow I had lost my ability to speak or move.

"Miss? Last stop."

Something made my chin move toward my chest in some kind of nod. And made me slowly, slowly stand up in my seat, gathering my knapsack onto my shoulders. I made my way up the aisle behind the driver.

One, two, my feet hit the ground. I shifted my knapsack higher as a tremor ran up and down my body. I was here.

Only, what was here, exactly?

Before me was a mass of confusion. Hundreds of voices seemed to be echoing off the walls and bouncing against one another, creating a low, busy hum. And the people—they were everywhere, walking fast and talking, walking and reading newspapers. Some wore dungarees and sweaters, like the folks back in Shadow Tree, but some wore fancy dresses, or dressy slacks and collared shirts, and then some were dressed outrageously—in great baggy pants or shiny silver jackets or coats with zippers and flaps everywhere. They all looked so different from one another, and so very different from me. I was still wearing my long blue dress, and it seemed out of place here—too flowy, too soft.

I had pictured this place so many times, but then the rushing quality I'd imagined had been kind of seamless and smooth. This was chaos. Without stopping, I made my way—and was half pushed as I stepped in front of one person after another—through the throngs of people and toward the nearest doorway. I felt compressed, squeezed like a lemon, and more than wanting to stare and stare, I wanted to get outside, where hopefully it wouldn't be so crowded.

I welcomed the cool breeze as if it was my first breath of air as the person ahead of me pushed through the door and I followed behind him. I was immediately confronted with a whole different set of sounds—honking, cars honking, I figured—far and wide, and roaring motors and steam zipping out of the edges of this strange metal circle, like a lid of some sort, on the ground to my left. What . . .

And then, my Lord, the buildings.

Every which way that was all there was, building upon building, no space between them. There wasn't a patch of grass to be seen from where I stood. Only glass and metal and bricks. Some that I could see in the distance were so big, they seemed to stretch clear to the sky. Nothing, not all the Boston stories in the world, not if I had sat with Mrs. Johansen for five years straight to hear them all, could have prepared me for this.

Boston wasn't a much bigger version of Shadow Tree, like I'd imagined it to be. It was another planet.

"Why don't they just tip over?" I muttered, really fearing that any moment the tallest buildings just might. They were impossible. Impossible. My head strained back and my neck stretched with it, far as it would go. My hat went tumbling off, and I let it lie.

I must have stood there gawking for ten minutes. I got bumped a few times, but any worries about strangers, or about looking too much like a stranger myself, vanished. My whole brain was taken up with wonder. And pride.

Katie, I am here. Do you see me? Was Katie with me? There was a weight in my stomach, there because Katie couldn't be here in person. But I could swear, imagination or no, that I felt her spirit right beside me. *We are going to do it all, all the things we dreamed of. I'm going to do it all—for both of us.*

Finally I scooped my hat up off the ground and removed my gloves. The air wasn't as cold as I'd expected. The sun peeked down from the holes in the sky left by the buildings, darting in and out of clouds and sending brief little slices of warm light onto the walkway where I stood. It wasn't a cold, sharp-as-glass day like when I'd come to Shadow Tree. It was the kind of day that invited you in. It matched my happiness.

Suddenly unable to stand still another minute, what with so much ahead, I waited for a car to go past, then drifted across the street, hardly looking where I was going, not stopping myself as I drifted farther and farther from the terminal and deeper into the city. I couldn't have stopped if I'd wanted to. My legs felt like they were on clouds. No, they felt like they *were* clouds.

There were people on every corner, trickling in groups or by themselves across each street, as far as the eye could see. Beautiful brick buildings bumped up against others that glinted and gleamed like they were made out of silver. A man stood behind a metal cart that was roiling with steam and smoke that drifted off the side and into my nostrils. It smelled divine. A closer look told me it was hot dogs—I remembered with a sad smile that they were one of the only foods little Andrew Aiden really liked. The streets were dirtier than I expected or would have ever pictured, and it all seemed looser somehow than I had imagined it—more unraveled—but I didn't care. It was all beautiful. Every single inch.

I walked in no real direction, down one street with a glint of light at the end, then another that beckoned to me with an inviting smell. Eventually my feet brought me into a giant courtyard paved all over with brick and lined with small buildings. It was like the city had suddenly become miniaturized and not so overwhelming, giving my eyes some relief and a bigger glimpse of the blue sky. The buildings lined a big open square and contained stores of all sorts, like Main Street in Shadow Tree, but bigger.

In the middle of it all was a giant house made of clear glass.

To me, it looked as sparkling and pure as something an angel would live in. Only, there were lots of people trickling out the front doors with bags of food in their arms. And some other people trickling in. On closer look, it seemed to be a market of some sort. Could it be?

I let myself melt into a crowd that was flowing in through the large doors and crossed my fingers, hoping I'd be allowed in. But nobody even noticed me or cared.

Inside, I caught my breath. A long aisle stretched down before me, crowded on both sides with stand after stand, each selling a different kind of food. There must have been forty or more stands. I started wondering if I could ever stop being surprised by Boston, even if I could live here for fifty years. It didn't seem possible, given the different worlds I'd seen in just a few hours so far.

The smells combined in the air—meats and spices and coffee and sweets—were divine. One stand sold pizza, which I remembered Becky had ordered for us once in Shadow Tree, over the telephone. Another sold sandwiches. Some sold food from countries I'd heard of—there was Chinese, Japanese, Greek. I'd never imagined that their food could look and smell so different.

Pizza was the only thing I could afford—a dollar-fifty a slice—and after a quick debate with myself (I longed to keep walking and to keep my money, but my stomach longed for food), I waited in line while the mustached man behind the counter served the folks ahead. When he got to me, I pointed at the plain kind with just cheese on top and said, "Two, please." And paid him out of the little stash of money (three dollars and thirty-eight cents) I had left.

Back outside and on the first empty bench I could find, I gobbled the first slice of pizza. As I chewed, I watched the people pass by—walking in or out of the glass building or shopping along the sides of the square. Some of them emerged with big colorful bags bulging with their purchases, and many were smiling as they moseyed around. They, too, seemed relieved that the weather had warmed a bit. And people here seemed more relaxed than those I'd seen at the bus station. But maybe this was how it always was in Boston, when they weren't trying to catch a bus headed away. Maybe people had so much at their fingertips, they never wanted for anything, and that was what made them look so comfortable and happy.

Hungry as I was, I decided to save my second slice for later and carefully wrapped it up in its bag. By that time the weather was getting colder, and the chill in the air made me remember that I still had to find a warm place to sleep for the night. "Shoot," I muttered, buttoning my coat. "Where do I even start?" I knew there was such a thing as hotels, but I knew I couldn't afford one. And I hadn't planned or thought up any other possibilities. *Fool, Glory.*

Dusk fell as I peered down one street after another, searching for a nook or hiding place of some sort. After what seemed like hours of looking and turning up no proper place, I realized I wasn't going to find anything on the streets. I was going to have to venture into a building of some sort. Only what sort? It had to be one where I wouldn't be seen.

I guess I must have already been thinking *church* before I saw it. All those years being told that church was a sanctuary from the cruel world (even though for me it'd always been a boring, stuffy building) must have sunk in. I'd passed a couple of what I thought were churches earlier that day, but I'd ignored them and the thoughts of God that came with them. Now, when I saw a cross towering above a brown stone building ahead, I hurried toward it hopefully. A soft light poured out through the cracks in a big wooden door that stood at the top of some steps.

"Suffer little children, and forbid them not to come unto me: for of such is the kingdom of heaven," I muttered. It came out of my mouth as naturally as breathing. Then, crossing my fingers, I walked up the stairs and stepped inside.

Whoa. Of all the things I'd seen today, could be this was the most perplexing of all. It was nothing like the church in Dogwood or even the one in Shadow Tree. The two sides of the roof raced up to meet each other and collided in intricate lines and patterns, carved deep into the stone. The walls were adorned with glass that split into several different colors, all as deep and rich and glossy as the gems in Becky's store. Three aisles led from where I stood—one, lined with benches, led to the front and another cross, illuminated from behind by white light; the others stretched off to either side of me and ducked around opposite corners, lined with white, graceful statues here and there.

It was truly stunning. And also gloomy, and serious, and solemn. It made no sense. Weren't Christians everywhere supposed to be humble? This place was fancy as could be. Maybe this was what the Reverend had always made such a fuss about. Maybe folks in the modern world had their values all mixed up.

From my spot at the back I could see one person half kneeling, half sitting in one of the benches near the front, her hands clasped together in prayer. I didn't go up the aisle toward her but turned left and then right, finding a corridor that ran parallel to the main aisle but that was hidden from it by more brown stone walls.

There were several doors along these walls, and when I tried them gently, they all turned out to be locked. My hope fading, I turned back and headed down a similar corridor on the other side, but again, not one door would budge. *Maybe I could sleep under one of the benches,* I thought desperately. Maybe I could squeeze under one and lie really still.

Just as I prepared to turn back again, I took a closer look at an alcove tucked away to my right. I'd assumed it was only a little indentation. But there, beside a statue of a man with his hands outstretched, was another door. I tried it, and this time it gave way, onto steep wooden stairs that spun their way upward. Casting a last look around the corridor, I closed the door behind me and silently climbed the steps, finally arriving at a little parapet-type space.

To my surprise, the parapet looked down upon the main aisle and the illuminated cross and the woman who still knelt praying at the front. There was only a tiny space of floor up here, but it was big enough for someone my size to sleep on. More than that, it was as good as I was going to get, and it was warm and dry. Thankful for my luck, I started making a bed on the floor out of my coat and knapsack. Once in a while I stole a glance down at the woman below, till she was finally gone.

"Thank goodness," I whispered, and yanked the leftover pizza out of my knapsack in a blink.

As I bit into the pizza, a clicking sound arose from downstairs. I stopped midbite. *Tap, tap, tap.* The slow, heavy footsteps—like a man's footsteps—echoed along the downstairs floor, sending gooseflesh up and down my arms. Up one corridor and down another, it sounded like, until it seemed they must be right underneath me.

I froze, holding the pizza to my lips and waiting, too scared to move my hands. I worried whoever it was might hear my heartbeat, it was so loud. *Click!*

Suddenly I was bathed in darkness. The lights had all gone off. I felt adrift, lost, frightened as I'd ever been. I'd wondered too many times what would happen if I got caught by some adult, someone who'd see I had no place to go.

I didn't dare breathe as the footsteps sounded again—but to my relief, they seemed to be headed away. Then came the creak of the heavy front door opening and slamming shut. And another click. And the footsteps sounded no more.

I waited for a few more minutes to make sure. Then, unable to hold my pose any longer, my shoulders collapsed, my pizza fell into my lap, and I let myself breathe in big, deep gasps. I wasn't hungry anymore.

Slowly I set the food aside and sat up so that my elbows leaned on the side of the parapet. For a few moments while I caught my breath, I watched the church glow dark red and blue and green, lit as it was by the streetlight, broken into different colors by the glass. Nothing moved. But then the statues, and the cross especially, seemed to take on a life of their own in that light, and it brought back my gooseflesh. There didn't seem to be any more people in here, but if there was such a thing as ghosts, they'd be sure to haunt a place like this.

With that thought I settled into my covers, where the only sound was my heart beating—*thump, thump, thump.*

CHAPTER
ELEVEN

The next morning brought cold, heavy rain that pelted me sideways. Of course, I didn't have a raincoat.

Wasn't it too cold to rain? In the mountains back home, we'd have never seen rain on a day like today. We would have seen white gusts of snow, falling in clouds of flakes that blew this way and that, at odds with one another. And anyhow, what had happened to the Boston of yesterday, all sunny and inviting?

Having carefully snuck my way out of the church a few minutes after the doors had been unlocked, I plodded on down the street, the moisture immediately seeping in through the tops of my shoes. *Shoot. Shoot shoot shoot.*

Before I'd even made it a full block in the hard rain, I retreated under a stone archway and huddled as far inside as I could get. Hands trembling with cold and hunger, I decided to ignore the rain for a moment and dug in my knapsack for my remaining slice of pizza from the night before. I pulled it out of the paper sack and . . .

No!

Oh, Glory. Oh, Glory, you fool.

My pizza landed facedown on the wet ground, in an indent

that ran down one side of the street. Still shivering, desperately now, I fished my remaining money out of my pocket. Thirty-eight cents. Oh, Lord. Oh, how was I going to eat?

The rain continued to pour down. Bitterly I reflected that my plans for this city had never included finding a way to eat. Or rain, for that matter, dumb as that was. Rain hadn't made its way into any of Mrs. Johansen's stories. And it scared me. Mama had always told me never to go out in the cold with a wet head, and now here I was, already soaked. I couldn't imagine the hat would do much good against this heavy rain. What if I got a cold? What would that do to me? Would I ever recover?

Without another thought, I turned and ran back toward the church and hurried inside. Whoever came to turn the lights on and off and unlock the doors was nowhere to be seen. I walked to one of the pews and sat, my teeth chattering and my hair sticking to the sides of my face, as a few other folks trickled in. The knot in my throat stayed awhile, curled up and made itself comfortable. My happiness of yesterday had reversed almost immediately, and I was in the blackest of moods. What had I done? What was I doing?

You've just got to focus, I told myself. Thinking to be practical, I pulled my Boston list out of my knapsack and looked it over. What could I get done today?

Swan boats, I read. It was too cold and rainy—Mrs. Johansen had said it was a warm-weather thing. *Eat in a restaurant?* I sighed, thinking the money I had wouldn't buy me *anything* to eat, much less a meal in a restaurant. I'd have to get to that later, somehow. I had no earthly idea where the church from Mrs. Johansen's picture was. And the newspaper . . . that would cost money, too. I didn't have even a little to spare. All at once I realized how hard doing the things on this list was going to be.

But I wouldn't worry about that now. I wouldn't worry about any of it. Because finally I spotted one thing on the list that I *could* do today. And I wanted to get started. I waited for the rain to die down and tried not to think about all the doubts taking over.

"Can I help you?"

I'd just made my way through the giant glass doors of the first skyscraper I'd happened upon. A man was standing in front of me, looking me up and down and seeming doubtful.

I strained to peer over his shoulder, to see what was behind him, but he shifted himself to block my view.

"I want to go to the top floor . . . sir," I said, clearing my throat first. Still, it came out in a squeak.

"Are you here for an appointment?" he asked, now losing his doubtful look and straightening up his shoulders, folding his hands. I could feel myself blushing. I thought of how I must appear, damp and scraggly with a dirty knapsack and no raincoat. But I plunged forward anyhow. Or tried.

"Uh, no, sir, I just . . ."

"Well, you need a visitor's pass," he said. I opened my

mouth to reply, but he kept going. "And for that you need to have an appointment with someone who works here."

"But I . . ." I wanted to say that I needed to do this. That he didn't understand how important it was. But the look on his face told me it was no use. It was a look that said I wasn't welcome.

"I . . . I'm sorry," I said, and before he could say another word, I hurried outside.

The drizzle I'd walked over in had turned into a light mist, and it felt blessedly cool against my burning face. Feeling frail and empty, I leaned into a nearby corner, wondering if I could try another building, ever. I felt humiliated, even though I hadn't done anything wrong. I guess the way he'd looked at me had struck a nerve. I felt like I had been pulling the wool over one pair of eyes after another—Jake, Becky, Becky's kids—I'd been so lucky. And now I'd suddenly come up against a stranger who saw me for what I was, a girl who didn't belong, who wasn't even worth his time.

I kicked at a tiny puddle that had formed near my feet, sending droplets splashing. Could be hunger was making me feel even more sour than I would have otherwise. One thing was sure, I couldn't imagine trying another skyscraper. Not today.

Absently I watched the people pass by, some of them slowing down to toss what all into a bin diagonally across the courtyard beside the building. They didn't look so happy and relaxed today, more grim, and tired, and intimidating. Maybe it was the rain. Maybe it was me.

My eyes glossed over as I looked at them, yet I stopped really paying attention. My vision got blurry with tears. I wasn't seeing Boston anymore. I was seeing home. I had a sudden longing for my mama, even more than the usual dull ache.

But then something started to nibble at the edges of my sadness. Something I was seeing. It took me a few minutes to realize what it was. Some of the stuff people were throwing away, in cups and bags and such, some of it was food.

I'd just seen a woman toss a half-covered sandwich of some sort into the bin, a bit of meat poking out from in between bread. I looked left to right. I made sure she was out of sight. Was I really going to do this? My stomach growled an answer.

In another moment I was leaning over the bin, digging for the sandwich. Joyfully I picked it up. It was only a tiny bit, and it was cold, but it was something. I started to pull away with my find, but then I noticed something else—a round white container, covered with a white top, pouring off steam. Warm steam.

Without a thought, I dropped the sandwich and picked up the container, ripping off the lid. I didn't even care if anyone saw me anymore. I didn't even bother to look up when a figure came into the corner of my vision. I was too intent on my treasure—a bowl, almost all the way full, of hot, creamy, white soup!

"That's spoiled." The voice had come from behind me. I whipped around to face a girl about my age, probably a little younger, her hands tucked deep in her raggedy coat, her face lined with dirt. She was different than most of the people I'd seen. Everything about her was worn and shabby. Even more than me. "I guess that's why they threw it away. Better steer clear."

I looked down at my soup, then back at the stranger in front of me.

"You better give that to me," she said, reaching out her hand. "It'll make you sick. Don't worry. I'll show you where to get some *real* food."

A battle was going on inside me. Should I get away from this stranger as quick as possible? Should I throw away my food, which I desperately wanted to eat? Should I talk to her? She was the first person who'd actually spoken to me nicely since I got here, and it would be a relief to talk to someone. Only, how did I know I could trust her?

She still had her hand stretched out as I looked down at the precious, hot soup again. It didn't look spoiled. When milk was spoiled, it curdled—but this looked fine. Well, there was only one way to find out. Still keeping my eyes on the girl, I took a sip. It tasted delicious.

"Thank you, anyway. I'm gonna keep it," I said, narrowing my eyes suspiciously. Clearly she had only wanted the perfectly good soup for herself.

The girl pulled back her hand and stared at me under heavy lids.

"You're not from around here, are you?"

I shook my head, clutching the soup to my chest as if she might lunge for it at any second.

"Don't worry," she said, shoving her hands deep inside her pockets. "I'm not gonna take your soup."

I tried my best at a friendly smile. She smiled back.

"Greta," she said, lifting up her hand in a half wave instead of putting it out to shake.

"I'm Glory," I said. "Pleased to meet you."

Greta's green eyes danced with amusement. "Nice accent," she said.

I looked down at my gloves, embarrassed. Was it that obvious, even among outsiders, that I was an outsider?

"You have a place to stay?" Greta asked, tilting her head to one side. She spoke quickly, in clipped little words that sounded strange to my ears. It made her sound extra smart somehow.

"Um, yes, I . . ." I trailed off.

"God, you don't have to be so shy. I'm not gonna bite you or anything. You look like you think I'm a spy."

"A spy?"

"I'm homeless, or whatever you wanna call it, just like you. I was just gonna give you some advice."

"Homeless?"

Greta didn't answer. She just gave me another long stare. "But I guess you've got it covered. Good luck. I'll see you later." Greta turned on her heel and headed away. My voice caught in my throat. Should I go after her? Was it safer to be on my own?

"Wait!" I hollered, hurrying up to her and holding out the soup container, offering her a sip. I had a strange feeling about Greta, but I definitely needed help, and she seemed to know how things worked out here. Greta, not looking at all surprised, grabbed the cup and took a long swig. "What kind of advice?" I asked.

Before answering, she handed me back the cup. It was completely empty.

Greta had been on the streets for three years, ever since she was nine. She wouldn't tell me how she'd ended up there or where she'd been before. She did say she'd been picked up by "the cops" twice—once for trying to break into a store, for clothes, she said, and once for going into a shelter for food.

"They hold these shelters out to you like they're candy," she said, "but if you're a kid, it's just a trap. They outed me to Child Welfare, then Child Welfare put me in a foster home. It was awful. The people just made me their personal slave. In two weeks I escaped and took the T back into the city." I nodded. It was the first proof I'd ever had about what Jake had told me way back before Shadow Tree. Not that I felt Greta was entirely believable. But she was the only source of advice I had now.

According to Greta, "foster parents" were people who got paid to keep children at their houses. She said ending up with these people was the worst thing that could happen to you.

She said they "exploited" you for money, whatever that meant, and made you do all sorts of things you didn't want to do.

As she explained all this, she took me around to different spots to search for food, explaining where the best garbage cans were for both the number of people throwing things out and the quality of food (like outside certain stores and even a café). Neither of us paid much attention to the sights I'd been so amazed at yesterday. I was too amazed by Greta alone.

And I was stunned by something else that Greta was revealing to me. The fact that there were other people like us— people with no home—here. Lots of them.

Every few corners I began to note folks poking through the trash. Some just dug right in, while others seemed to want to keep it secret. But now I saw these folks everywhere. They were usually looking downward, like the weight of the world rested on their shoulders. Some of the men had bushy, dirty beards. Many of the women were scraggly haired and stooped.

"Stay away from her," Greta said, gesturing to one lady carrying a large, black bag full of who knew what. "She'll talk your ear off if you let her. She's nuts." Then she pointed to her head and waggled her finger. Every once in a while she'd make another comment about somebody else. I was too confused to press her on any subject. It was all so darn hard to understand.

Finally the day started to darken, and my soul seemed to sink at the idea of saying good-bye to Greta. I didn't trust her, but at least I was beginning to feel I knew what to expect from her. What if there were other strangers here who were capable of far worse? The idea of being all alone for the night made me shiver. But when we swung back by the place where we'd met earlier, Greta stopped and looked at me expectantly.

"So're you gonna come to the yards with me?"

"The yards?"

Greta tilted her head at me, looking slightly annoyed. "You do need a place to sleep, don't you? You were lying before."

"Oh," I muttered, embarrassed. "Oh, well, I'm . . ."

"Don't worry about it," Greta said, then seeing my look of doubt, she softened into a smile. "Showing you the yards is the least I can do."

A mixture of relief and fear washed over me. Greta was gonna take me with her. She didn't even mind that I had lied. I didn't get that feeling—like I had with Jake and Becky—that I could trust her. But what other choice did I have?

We twisted down several streets on a path to God knew where. My eyes felt itchy and dry, and my head had a tiny bit of the swimminess it had had on the bus, but I didn't much notice it. Finally we reached a doorway that led to some stairs going down to an underground corridor.

I marveled at the inside. There were no windows at all; we were completely underground. People were rushing to and fro, and beeping and clicking sounds filled the air. "You go first,"

Greta said, interrupting my staring and pointing to a three-pronged metal thing ahead of us. "I'll look out."

I looked at Greta in confusion, and she looked back at me, her forehead scrunched up with impatience.

"Well?" she asked. "Go on, jump it."

I bit my bottom lip and stared at the metal contraption. Someone ahead of me dropped a tiny coin in a slot beside it and then pushed on through. But something told me that wasn't what Greta was suggesting. Finally, with a great sigh, she walked ahead of me, planted both hands on either side of the contraption, and hopped over. She kept going, not even looking back. I peered around, knowing deep down we weren't supposed to be doing this but desperate not to lose Greta, especially here, underground. Then, having no other choice, I bit my lip and did the same. And we were on our way.

I about keeled over as we watched the train, the "T," Greta called it, come hurtling toward us down the tracks. I fought the urge to grab Greta's arm and pull her backward, but she grabbed my elbow and pulled me forward. "We wanna get a seat," she said. "It's rush hour." I knew about trains but had never seen one up close and had never imagined one that went underground. If Greta hadn't been here, I would have turned tail and taken my chances with the church or somewhere out on the streets.

We were the first ones on when the train came to a stop and the doors opened. Greta yanked me into the nearest seats as I gaped about like a fish out of water, absorbing the crowd, the long, white lights, the walls lined with pictures. There was one picture of a carton of orange juice. There was another of a man sitting at a desk, with writing below that talked about how you could take classes to become a "computer technician." The train stopped several times, people trickling in and out, before Greta motioned me to get up. I was ill at ease the entire time.

After following another underground corridor like the one we'd come in through, we emerged into the outer world. It was dark now, but I could see by the streetlights that we were in a very different part of the city—if we were still *in* the city. The buildings were much, much lower here and less beautiful. In fact, they looked forgotten. Many windows were broken, some walls were crumbling, but many seemed to have people inside. I trailed behind Greta silently and tried to take her lead. She didn't look scared at all, so I tried not to, either. Finally we came to a metal fence, and Greta squeezed through a small opening, pulling it wide behind her so I could squeeze through, too.

We were in a train yard of some sort. I could tell because there were tracks along the gravelly ground and then a few darkened, abandoned cars like the one we'd come on. Their windows had been completely poked or smashed out. They were covered in painted words scrawled here and there. And then there were people. Lots of them.

They were hunkered down in front of a few small fires. Some

were asleep and some were muttering, either to themselves or one another. One lady was moaning loudly. Mostly, though, they were silent, a group that didn't seem to notice one another but huddled together like a herd of deer for safety. Their clothes, their faces—everything about them was ragged and worn down. Even I could see this place was filled with misery.

This . . . this was worse than anything the Reverend had ever described. He had talked about people being selfish and greedy. He'd never conjured up a picture of so many lost souls living, well, what couldn't even be called lives. It had been more comforting to think that I was the only one or maybe one of a few.

How many people were there like this? How had they come to this? I'd deserved being cast out. Had they?

Greta led me on a twisted path through one pitiful group after another, finally jumping into one of the train cars and holding out her hands to help me up behind her. I crinkled up my nose at the smells of dirty clothes and dirty bodies wafting out to me. A lump of a man was asleep on the left.

"I'm way at the back," Greta said, stomping along in the shadowy car and finally stopping at the end. She pointed to a pile at her feet—a few blankets, a black garbage bag. "For when it rains," she said, noticing my horrified stare.

I wished Greta hadn't brought me here. I wished I hadn't seen this.

"You can share my space," she said, not seeming bothered

at all. She was shuffling around in the dark, arranging our "bed." "I'm gonna go out and warm up by the fire for a while. Maybe you should just sleep."

She didn't have to argue me into it. I just wanted to close my eyes and forget I was here. And I wanted to stay out of sight. Who knew what these people were like or what kind of things they would do? I'd try to stay as invisible as possible.

It took a long time to get to sleep, but I must've finally done it because I didn't hear Greta when she came back in. I only heard my knapsack being opened and blinked in confusion as I saw Greta, outlined by the moonlight and not noticing I was awake, leaning over my bag and shuffling through my belongings.

My heart thumped loudly in my chest. My skin ran hot and cold. Was Greta . . . stealing from me? Lying to me about soup I had found so she could have it was one thing, but taking things that *belonged* to me was something I could not even comprehend.

I lay still as a statue. For all the world, I didn't want her to know what I was seeing. I was ashamed for her. And for me, for being so easily lied to. I wanted to cry. Finally someone was proving the Reverend right. I should have . . .

Then I thought of my photo, and with that I jerked upright. Greta jerked with me.

"Glory!" she whispered, though she didn't need to since I was awake.

"Greta?" I said. "What . . . ?"

Greta stretched one hand toward me as she replied, "I thought you were asleep, and I needed matches. To get a fire going."

Now it came into focus. The hand she was holding toward me held my box of matches, the one that Jake had given me. It took me a few seconds to understand. *Oh.* My shoulders sagged with relief, but a tiny speck of distrust still zipped up and down my nerves. "I'm sorry . . ." I started to say.

"Don't worry—you're just jittery. No big deal. So can I borrow these?" she said, indicating the matches again.

"Uh, sure . . ." I said. "I . . ."

But Greta was already up and backing out of the car.

When she was gone, I thought of lying back down, but instead I stood to peer through one of the broken-out windows of the train car. Greta was walking across the lot, toward a trash can with a few other people around it. It was already leaping with flames.

She sat down, casually slipped the matches into her coat pocket, then rubbed her hands together.

She didn't use them to light anything. She didn't use them at all.

CHAPTER TWELVE

Greta was gone when I awoke. I stumbled out of the train car into the sunlight, but there was no sign of her anywhere. Bleary-eyed, I wiped at my face with my sleeve.

A scraggly, bearded man was sitting by one of the fires—the flames licking out the top of a big metal container. I nervously stepped up beside him, placing my fingers near the fire for warmth. I wondered about Greta, about what I had seen and what I should think. I wondered if folks here were all thieves and bad people and that's why they'd ended up here in the first place.

"You came in with Greta last night."

I jumped at the sound of the man's voice. It seemed to have come from someone else. This man looked like he'd have the voice of a grizzly bear, but the words had come out soft and refined.

"She's already gone downtown," he said. He hadn't looked at me. He was still staring into the fire. Then he hauled his large form off the ground, seeming to forget I was there at all. And then he was walking away. I panicked. I didn't know how to get back to the main part of the city, and I didn't know how to find food here. The hunger was already gnawing at me. I stood up and hurried after the man.

"Um, sir, are you going into town, too?" I asked. The man didn't look back, but he seemed to nod. "Do you mind if I come along?"

This time he didn't even nod, but having no other choice, I took it as a yes. I followed several feet behind him, out of the yards, down the strange, sad streets Greta and I had come by, wondering if he even knew I was there. The only indication he gave was one backward glance before disappearing into the train station. I hurried to keep up.

We didn't say a word on the train. I let myself be mesmerized again by the giant pictures on the walls and all the people. There were more folks on this one train car than in the entire town of Dogwood, it seemed.

When the man I was following started to get off at one of the stops, I went to get off, too, only suddenly I was being smushed on all sides by people. I couldn't breathe. I couldn't see! I was swept off the train, and when I finally had room to look around, I didn't see any sign of my guide. He had disappeared. Shoot.

I hadn't even memorized the way back to the yards. How would I get back? What would I do if I couldn't?

I let myself drift with the crowd, up the stairs and out into the morning. At least the sun was out again. At least I had that going for me. And the buildings and the cars—they were still stunning and overwhelming and beautiful.

I started walking in the direction I happened to be facing, beginning my search for breakfast.

Luckily I managed to find a full meal—two hamburgers and fried potatoes—early on. I was so full afterward, I couldn't think of foraging anymore, so I pulled out my list of things to do in Boston. Again I didn't have the means to do any of them but one, and I just couldn't bring myself to try another skyscraper. Not now.

Listlessly I wandered about, getting farther and farther away from the area I'd been haunting for the past two days. I shuffled past pretty brick buildings and little brick houses lined up in rows. And then, out of nowhere, appeared a big, grassy field. I had to rub my eyes to make sure I wasn't imagining it.

Not only was there grass everywhere—much greener than March weather should allow—but there was a pond in the middle and a few ducks floating in that pond, their feathers white as snow and their beaks bright yellow. How they got to this pond in the middle of the city, I couldn't imagine. A sign poking its way out of the grass to eye level said Heritage Park.

Gosh, it was a sight for sore eyes. I hadn't realized how much I'd missed nature in the past few days. It felt like a rest for my eyes and my soul—something familiar, something that didn't feel so strange and overwhelming. I made my way over to a bench and sat, hoping that I was allowed.

A smell drifted up to me that I had almost forgotten—a wet dirt smell. I breathed it in greedily. It smelled like home. It smelled like this day last year when Katie and Theo and I had gone foraging for salamanders in the woods. It smelled so good, I figured I could sit here forever, I could wait to die right here. Or at the very least stay for a day or two. If there wasn't so much to do. And so little time to do it in.

One of the ducks now climbed out of the pond and wad-dled up to within a couple of feet of me, bobbing his head from side to side and looking like he expected something. Food. I raised my hands, palms up. "I don't have anything."

The duck kept on looking at me and quacking. I stared back.

"You don't get it, huh?" I asked. "Me neither. I don't get anything."

I laughed. But it wasn't a real laugh. It was a bitter one. Then I burst into tears.

What was I doing? Was I crazy? How was I going to do this? How was I ever going to do any of the things I'd planned to do when I couldn't even plan where my next meal would come from? How was I supposed to make anything up to Katie when I had gotten myself into such a mess? Swan boats? Eating in fancy restaurants? How could those things ever happen?

The truth of it all came over me. The only way I could see

from here was down. Sicker, and poorer, and dirtier, and worse. Like Greta. And the folks in the yards. It wasn't what I'd come here for. It wasn't anything close to what Katie and I had planned and what I had promised to follow through on. I was failing. All this way, and I was still failing her.

"Glory?"

I don't know how long I'd been slumped on my bench.

"I've been looking for you. What's wrong?" Greta was sitting right next to me. *Could* Greta be sitting right next to me? She put her hand on my shoulder and gave me a push.

"This place remind you of Alabama or Tennessee or wherever the heck you're from? Bringing back old Dixie memories?"

I was sitting up straight now, trying to understand that Greta had found me, wanting to ask what she was talking about.

"The matches," I answered instead, wiping at my eyes.

"Don't tell me you're stuck on that?" Her green eyes narrowed at me, but one corner of her lips turned up.

I sniffed and stared back at her. With a flourish she pulled out the box of matches and handed them back to me. "Here, if it's such a big deal."

Lowering my eyes, I took the matches and tucked them into my knapsack. "It's, uh, it's not a big deal," I said, feeling foolish yet again. She was looking at me so clearly and kindly. She'd searched for me. She couldn't be all that bad.

"Good," Greta said, giving me another light shove on the shoulder. "Wanna get going?"

"Get going where?"

"Home, dummy," she said, raising her arms to indicate the world around us. It was getting dark, clearly time to head out. Lights had started appearing—some in clusters, some on their own—in the buildings of the city. Like diamonds. Far away, but beautiful all the same.

"Yeah," I said to Greta, feeling the disappointment and fear ease, for a while. "Yeah, I'm ready."

When I woke, it was blackness. And Greta, once again, was rifling around the car. If she was in my knapsack again, I'd . . .

"Greta," I said, kneeling up in my covers. "What are you . . . ?"

But now that I was up, I realized it wasn't quite blackness in the car. There was a white light shooting across the windows, illuminating Greta's figure for a second. Her movements were panicked and rushed. That's when I noticed the voices coming from outside—yelling—and a loud, shrill whistle.

Wide awake now, I shot up to the window and could make out, by the dying fires and the streams of light fanning this way and that, that the inhabitants of the settlement were running everywhere, being chased and scattered by people in dark uniforms. Oh, God. In my very bones, I knew it was the police.

I felt a hand on my collar, pulling me away from the opening.

"What are you doing!?" It was Greta, glaring at me. "You're gonna get us both caught." Then she turned and began crawling toward the open doorway. I only took a moment to grab my knapsack, then I followed right behind her, not caring whether she wanted me with her or not.

Outside it was chaos, people running this way and that, grabbing their meager bundles of belongings, racing through chinks in the fences surrounding us.

Greta and I ducked as another ray of light shot toward our car, then disappeared. My whole body felt as soft as pudding. My bones and muscles felt like they had melted away. Fear had replaced everything.

Following Greta's lead, I ran to the next train car over, flattening my back against it. From where we stood, I could see four or five police people, wielding gleaming clubs. Beyond them—about twenty-five yards yonder—was the hole in the fence through which Greta and I had come. I figured surely that was where she meant to go. Only there was no place to hide in between here and there.

My eyes shut tight for a moment, then opened again. I heard the crunch of gravel behind me. Greta and I both turned into the glare of a light shining in our eyes.

And then we ran. Leaping over debris and not looking to either side—just heading for that hole in the fence. We could make it.

We were halfway across when a large figure appeared in front of us. What happened next was a blur. Greta, who was leading, doubled backward in a flash. The next moment her hands were on me, and then I was tumbling forward. Right into the arms of the figure. I didn't think; I just struggled. I managed to turn enough so that I could see Greta duck and disappear through the far fence without a backward glance.

Finally I looked up to see who, exactly, was holding me. The man staring down at me had a mustache and dark hair. He had arms as strong as steel that wouldn't let me budge. He had a flashlight in his other hand, and on his chest was a big, shiny badge.

My mind began to focus, and everything became clear all at once. Greta had pushed me. To save herself, Greta had pushed me . . . right into the arms of the police.

It was a lot like this movie Amelia and I had watched on the television. The room was buzzing with voices and the hum of what I knew by now were computers being used, folks typing on the keys. The lights were bright and white and uncomfortable because they offered no place to hide. The policeman, Officer Greene, leaned over his desk and talked into a shiny black phone. I sat in a chair before the desk, my legs tucked under the seat, my arms crossed over my chest, like that could protect me.

"Okay, Lee, well, we'll keep waiting to hear," was what he was saying. Was this a nightmare?

Officer Greene hung up the phone and looked at me severely. "That was Levi Bushfield," he said. "You know him." He didn't say it as a question. I didn't reply. I'd heard them talking. I knew how Mr. Bushfield had sent the police folks here in Boston a description of me. I knew now what a mistake it had been to tell Becky and the others I was trying to get to Boston.

"We can't match your fingerprints, Glory," Office Greene said. "So we can trace you to Shadow Tree, but no farther." He paused and waited. I didn't say a thing.

"What I'm saying is, we don't know where you're from or who you belong to. Officially you don't have an identity. And what happens if we can't find one for you is that you go to Child Welfare until they can place you in foster care. Understand?"

I understood. I understood what Jake, and later Greta, had told me about what would happen if I got caught. I shivered.

"The family you stayed with in Shadow Tree, the Aidens, is it? They're interested in adopting you. But if that's what you're hoping for, I gotta tell you not to hold your breath. The state appoints a suitable foster home for you, you understand? One where a local social worker can keep an eye on you.

"Now, Glory," Officer Greene said, not giving me time to reply. I would have said I wouldn't go back to the Aidens, anyway. I wouldn't leave Boston if there was any possibility I could stay. "You have another option. You can tell us the truth. You can tell us where you're from, who your parents are. You can tell us where you belong. We know this much—we know you don't belong in Boston."

I bit my lip. I felt the familiar feeling of my stomach flip-flopping inside me and wondered for the millionth time what was causing it—my own heart or the sickness. I didn't want any part of "Child Welfare" or "foster care" or anything. I wanted to be in Boston, and free, and somehow find a way to fulfill my promise.

I wanted to do the best thing for Katie and me. How could I do that locked away somewhere?

I'm so sorry, Katie, I said in my mind. *I'm so sorry I messed this up.*

Officer Greene said I had two choices, but the way I saw it, I had none. I could do one impossible thing—let them take me home to Dogwood, where I longed to be but where I could never be again, where I didn't even exist anymore—or let them take me to a foster home, where I'd live out the last of my days trapped like a canary in a cage, bound to who knew what kind of people.

Still, while it was a choice between a rock and a hard place, it was a decision that needed to be made.

I raised my eyes to the man sitting in front of me. I sucked in my breath. And then I said: "I have no family, sir. Do what you have to do with me."

EPILOGUE

We're riding down a street in Brookline, which is supposed to be a "suburb" of Boston. Sherry, my social worker, is sitting beside me. She gives me a pat on the shoulder, then leaves her hand there.

Sherry is nothing like I expected when they turned me over to Child Welfare. The modern world keeps surprising me—in bad ways and good. Bad because I got caught. Bad because Boston is bigger and tougher than I expected. Bad because of Greta—how she lied and used me to save her own skin. But good because Child Welfare was nothing like Greta's stories. Good because Sherry is good. She makes me feel safe. So far, I've met more good people than bad. That was a surprise, but it gives me hope.

It's strange, I know, to talk about hope when my life is running out so fast. And when I haven't done one thing I set out to do. But as we drive, I can see the houses on either side of me are with gingerbread latticework just like the Johansens', only painted in these bright, warm, colors. And it adds to my hope, makes me look forward to seeing these houses every day, for as long as I'm here.

Of course, I know the houses don't mean anything. My foster parents—the Kellys—may turn out to be as horrible as Greta warned me foster parents could be. But maybe they won't. Maybe Greta was lying about that, too. Maybe they are good people. Maybe it will feel like being in a home. Maybe, if I'm lucky, they can even help with what I need to do.

We pull to a stop in front of a "sky blue Victorian." That's what Sherry calls it. She steps out of the car and comes around the other side to open the door for me since I can't seem to think of moving.

I manage to step out and let myself be pulled along a stone walkway There's a lawn that is just beginning to green, and a tiny garden that is just beginning to sprout. In the garden there's a small stone creature—a little man with big pointy ears—and he grins at me. I have no earthly idea what to think of him.

But it doesn't matter because we're already up on the porch and Sherry has turned toward me. She has green eyes and she focuses them on me as she puts a hand on each of my shoulders. "You ready?" she asks, looking encouraging and maybe half sorry. Like she understands how strange and messy and scary this could be.

I smile back at her. It's fake, but it's something. It's what Jake would call my "game face." It's what Daddy would call my "mannerly young lady face."

I want to pray to God that the Kellys will be kind and not at all like Greta's stories. I want to confide in Him how scary it is, how everything depends on them, how the rest of my life rests in their hands. I would if I could forgive Him. It's the next and final part of my life, behind this door. It seems too important to leave to chance. But for now there's nothing else I can do.

"I'm ready," I say. Of course, I will never, ever be ready.

Don't miss

BLUE GIRL

the next gripping chapter in Glory's life

As the year moves from a harsh winter to a hopeful spring, Glory finds herself in a home once again. It's not the one she left behind in Dogwood, but it is a place where she feels safe and can concentrate on what she has set out to do for Katie.

Sent to a big, modern school, Glory is forced to fend for herself in a new way: she must learn the ways of other kids her age, while maintaining the secrets she holds of her past and her slowly dwindling future. This proves more difficult than she imagined when she meets Joe Trew. Joe is interested in Glory and her unusual ways, and he makes it clear that he'd like to get to know her better.

But the poison seems to be taking its toll on Glory. Her symptoms are getting worse day by day, and as much as she'd like a friend, she knows her time is running out. Friends are just not an option for Glory Mason.